Finding Langston

by LESA CLINE-RANSOME

Holiday House / New York

HOLIDAY HOUSE is registered in the U.S. Patent and Trademark Office.
Printed and bound in July 2020 at Maple Press, York, PA, USA.
www.holidayhouse.com
First Edition
9 10

Library of Congress Cataloging-in-Publication Data

Names: Cline-Ransome, Lesa, author.
Title: Finding Langston / by Lesa Cline-Ransome.
Description: First edition. I New York : Holiday House, [2018] I Summary:
Discovering a book of Langston Hughes' poetry in the library helps
Langston cope with the loss of his mother, relocating from Alabama to
Chicago as part of the Great Migration, and being bullied.
Identifiers: LCCN 2017030385 I ISBN 9780823439607 (hardcover)
Subjects: I CYAC: Books and reading—Fiction. I Poetry—Fiction. I Moving,
Household—Fiction. I Bullying—Fiction. I African-Americans—Fiction.
Single-parent families—Fiction. I Chicago (Ill.)—History—20th
century—Fiction.
Classification: LCC PZ7.C622812 Fin 2018 I DDC [Fic]—dc23 LC record available at
https://lccn.loc.gov/2017030385

"Homesick Blues," "One-Way Ticket," "Evenin' Air Blues," "Daybreak in Alabama,"
"Poem [4]," "Ardella," "The Negro Mother," and "Red Clay Blues" from
THE COLLECTED POEMS OF LANGSTON HUGHES by Langston Hughes,
edited by Arnold Rampersad with David Roessel, Associate Editor, copyright © 1994 by
the Estate of Langston Hughes. Used by permission of Alfred A. Knopf, an imprint of the
Knopf Doubleday Publishing Group, a division of Penguin Random House LLC. All rights
reserved. Any third party use of this material, outside of this publication, is prohibited.
Interested parties must apply directly to Penguin Random House LLC for permission.

Note to Readers

You may notice that Langston and his father, Henry, use the term colored,
while the librarians use the term Negro. The distinction is intentional and
demonstrates the divide that existed at the time between the older
traditions of the South and the racial progress of the North.

ISBN 978-0-8234-4582-0 (paperback)

For Kathy White, we love hard

*In memory of Michael White (1984–2017),
friend, son, artist*

one

NEVER really thought much about Alabama's red dirt roads, but now, all I can think about is kicking up their dust. I miss the hot sun on the back of my neck and how now the racket of cicadas, seems like no sound at all. At the end of a school day, 'fore I had to get home and do my chores, I could take my time walking just as slow as I pleased without someone pushing past and cutting their eyes like I was a stray dog come asking for scraps.

The school bell rings loud and I remember I'm a long way from Alabama, dirt roads, and slow walking. I grab my satchel and make my way fast down the stairs, through the school yard, past block after block of the cracked sidewalks of Chicago's South Side. I step quick past Binga State Bank, the Jackson Funeral Home, and Saul's Butcher Shop with rows of baloney lined up in the window like a curtain. I wish it were home I was rushing to. Instead, I'm hurrying to get as far away as I can from Haines Junior High School.

I sidestep a group of loud-talking women outside the Luxe Beauty Parlor, and a tired old man with round shoulders. Just like in Alabama, folks here are in all shades of brown, so many they call this part of Chicago the Black Ghetto, or the Black Belt. But of all the names this place is called, I love the name Bronzeville. A place filled with people, each one some color of bronze.

Finally I reach 4501 Wabash Avenue. At my building I sit on the stoop and catch my breath, waiting before I have to climb the broke-down stairs and walk hallways smelling like two-day-old garbage and fried onions. Waiting alone for Daddy in our kitchenette apartment. Landlord calls it an apartment but it ain't nothing but a room tucked in between and on top of a lot of other rooms. Nothing here belongs to us, just whoever pays the rent. The two beds, two old rickety chairs, one table, the bureau missing a drawer—nothing. And walls covered by the last tenant with old newspapers to hide the holes. When we first moved in I tried to read the headlines but there's so many layers, all I could make out was a few words and pieces of dates: *July 12…November 7… 1945.* Didn't really matter 'cuz news from a year or two ago ain't really no news at all.

This room is so small, it feels like I'm being squeezed from all sides. Daddy ain't the best company, but ain't nothing worse than being alone. Not used to coming home to an empty house. The smell of last night's dinner and Daddy's sweaty work clothes hanging in the air. Every day I open the door, it takes just a minute 'fore I remember I won't hear Mama getting supper started, or hear her humming—*His eye is on the sparrow, and I know He watches me*—and just a little bit longer to remember I won't see Mama ever again.

Our downstairs neighbor comes out, her two kids hanging tight to her. Looks like she's got one more on the way. The one in her arms is crying so loud, I gotta cover my ears. Daddy says folks in the North like to keep to themselves, so I guess that's why they never speak. I wouldn't know what to say if they did. Been here months now, and we still only know one neighbor by name. Sometimes I wish we didn't. Miss Fulton comes up the steps, struggling with a bag.

"Come help me," she says when she sees me sitting. Looks like I'll be going inside after all. Her plump hands pass me her bag. She lives on the top floor, across from us, and only time she talks to me is when she's asking for my help. More like *telling* me to help. *Get over here* and *I need you to . . .* I don't think she even knows my name. In Alabama I was raised on *please* and *thank you*. Ain't no way Miss Fulton's from Alabama.

Daddy says she's a teacher in a high school across town. Bad as my classroom is, I'd hate to be in hers. She's just about my mama's age, just as pretty, but she's as wide as my mama was narrow. Her freckled light skin nothing like my mama's smooth nutbrown. Mean as my mama was kind. And she's missing Mama's gap-toothed smile. "Uppity" is what folks back home would call her. And other words I ain't got no business thinking.

Following her up the stairs, I can barely see around her wide behind, swaying from one side to the other. She puffs all the way up the four flights. Every once in a while she stops to catch her breath.

"You okay, Miss Fulton?" I ask, almost wishing she don't make it to the top floor.

"Mmm-hmmm," she answers, grabs onto the rickety bannister and keeps on going. Me right along behind her.

Miss Fulton takes her sweet time getting her key out her purse, like I ain't standing there with heavy groceries. Finally, she opens the door, and I barely make it to the kitchen table.

"Careful with my things!" she says, loud.

"Yes ma'am," I say, half dropping the bag.

I look around wishing our apartment were this neat. It's only one room, with a small table pushed against a wall with flowery oilcloth spread on it. Smells like the lavender that grew along the edge of our road back home. A lace curtain hangs at the window and pictures of people with smiling faces in frames hang above the table. Daddy keeps a picture in his wallet of him and Mama all dressed up. He'll show if I ask. And if he's in the mood for showing. The other corner of the room has her bed and quilt, bright with patches of color. Even with the big stove that sits in the middle, black and ugly with who knows how many years of other folks' grease and dirt cooked in, it still feels like a home. Like what I used to have.

"Good day, ma'am," I say, backing out of the front door 'fore she finds something else for me to do.

I pull the key to our apartment out of my shoe and wriggle it in the lock. After I lost two 'cuz of the holes in my pants pockets, Daddy said I lose another, I just wait outside till he gets home. The metal scrapes my foot all day, but least I'm not waiting outside. Back home, never had a key. The door stayed open. Every day in Chicago makes it harder to remember Alabama. Like a candle fighting to stay lit in the wind. But I do remember the porch and the front door with no lock, creaky on rusty hinges. And of course I remember Mama, pulling me in close and burying her nose in my hair soon as I walked in the door.

I pull a chair up to the window and watch the goings-on downstairs. Bet there's more action on my street than in Cab Calloway's show at the Regal Theater on Saturday night. The cart man rolls by with his busted wagon collecting trash and tossed-out furniture. Two soldiers stroll past, looking like they're still on duty when everyone knows the war ended a year ago. Jackie and Shirley from school are turning the ropes for double Dutch on the sidewalk. *"Here comes Sally, sittin' in the alley,"* they sing to two girls in the middle jumping fast. Shirley's ponytail bobs in time to the ropes hitting the sidewalk. Jackie looks bored with her head tilted to the side, eyeing boys passing by. Some people are moving in across the street. The mother wears a dress too thin for the weather, reties her head-rag and lifts her two young ones out of a truck onto the sidewalk while a tall, skinny man and his boy, just about my age, untie the chairs and pots and everything else they own from the back of the truck. The boy looks as scared as I did the day we moved into 4501 Wabash.

Daddy comes walking tired and slow from the el train that rides on a track above the city. He nods to folks as he passes. He's so tall, folks gotta look up to see his face. Some nod back, some keep walking. I move the chair back and shut the window. By the time Daddy opens the door, my books are open wide and spread across the table. I take out my pencil and pretend I'm doing my schoolwork.

two

I like being the first in the classroom each morning so I can walk through the school yard and hallways 'fore most everyone arrives and 'fore the trouble starts. Means I gotta get up early with Daddy, ahead of the rest of the tenants, to get into the bathroom 'fore all the hot water is used up. If I'm slow getting up, I gotta wait in line. Folks complain every morning 'bout how many got to share it and people taking too long to do their business and how some folks got nasty habits. But for me and Daddy, it's our first time with an indoor toilet. And a sink with water running though my fingers like a river. I don't miss toting water from the well in a bucket for Mama to cook or clean with, or washing up from a basin in the corner of the room. Saturday nights was the only time we had hot water, in a tin tub filled to the brim with the water Mama heated for my bath.

Never had a toilet to flush in the outhouse. When I first came to Chicago, I pretended to have to go to the bathroom just to flush the toilet and watch the water spin in circles down a little hole. Daddy found out and fussed nearly all day 'bout *being wasteful*. A *sin*, he said. Been here two months now, but still can't get enough of that water, one spout for hot, one for cold. I make a cup with my hands and move them side to side to make the water just the right amount of both to wash up.

I get to school earlier than nearly everyone in my class and sit at the front nearest to my teacher, Mrs. Robins, where I can pretend I don't hear the laughing and talking in back of me. Mrs. Robins act like she doesn't hear it either, 'cause she sure doesn't stop it.

My schoolmates come in one by one.

"Hey, country boy!" someone says as they pass my desk. *Country boy*'s been my name since I came to Chicago. The name everyone in class says when they point at my run-over shoes and laugh at the overalls I still wear. And the way I speak. Sometimes Mrs. Robins will ask me to repeat my words, and that's when the whispers and laughs behind start up. Even when I know the answer to questions, I don't raise my hand. I'm still waiting on Daddy to buy me pants and a belt, and shoes that ain't worn through the soles, so I can look like the boys here in the North. The day stretches longer than an Alabama road and I do my best to pay attention, but I'm really just waiting for the bell to ring.

"Need any help today, Miss Robins?" I ask on my way out of the classroom.

"Not today, hon," she says, turning off the lights to go home.

I take my time walking down the stairs, running my hands 'long the cinder-block walls and stopping to tie my shoes. I duck into the bathroom to wash my hands even though there ain't a speck of dirt on them. Finally I open the door that leads out onto the school yard. It's empty. Quiet. I'm safe. The door closes behind me with a click, but before I get three steps into the yard I see them. All three of them. Standing with their backs against the wall waiting. For me.

Lymon's the leader. No quite tall as me, but thin as a rail. Got one eye a little smaller than the other. But not too small to see me from a mile away.

I ignore him. "Keep to yourself," Daddy always says, "and you'll stay out of trouble."

First shove hits me square in the back.

"You ingorin' me?" Erroll and Clem start laughing. They're not as mean as Lymon, but they're tryin'. Lymon does the talkin', they do the laughin'. Kinda like a preacher preaching the gospel and the congregation shoutin' *"Amen."* I heard Lymon once bothered a boy so bad, he left Haines and started in a school 'cross town. No chance Daddy moving me to another school. Course he never seen Lymon, Erroll, and Clem working me over from the time I get to school till the time I go home.

I ain't sure, but I'm willing to bet their families came from the South just like mine. Bet their mamas and daddies' words tumble out slow and lazy just like mine. Bet they worked fields with a plow and a mule just like mine. Outside school, I've seen some of the kids from my school walking with their families, and something about the way they talk and laugh a little too loud tells me they ain't been here as long as they like folks at school to believe. Some folks forget where they came from soon as they step off the train at Union Station.

We left Alabama in the hottest month of the year. Months after the sweet-smelling magnolia buds appeared on the trees, and right after we buried Mama. At her funeral, I stood at Mama's grave holding Grandma's hand and we sang "His Eye Is on the Sparrow" and "Precious Lord, Take My Hand" and all her favorite hymns right along with the choir who came from church. Sang loud enough so no one would notice Daddy's lips weren't moving.

Back at the house, folks from church piled my plate with potato salad and fried chicken and told me, "Sit down, baby, and eat," but for the first time ever, I couldn't make myself swallow a bite. I sat in the corner watching people filling up the rooms where Mama used to. Everywhere I looked I saw her sewing or soaking her feet or laughing with Daddy or fixing me breakfast. After everyone went on home and all the food was put away, Mama stayed with me in that house. I guess that's why barely one week later Daddy made me wear my itchy, hot Sunday clothes to the train depot. Sweat ran down my back till it tickled. Me and Daddy squeezed into the last seats near the engine. So many people, some folks had to stand. In the colored section, we could smell the smoke and the air was thick. The white car was at the end of the train, folks said with plenty of seats and air clean and fresh. A curtain separated the colored car from the white, and only the porters and the conductor could pass through.

I can't think about all that now. Not with Lymon on my heels. I walk faster.

Back home I had friends. Not a lot, but enough to make me feel like I fit. At lunch, outside, we'd play marbles together, sometimes climb the tree in back of the school. No one laughed when I talked, or pointed at my run-over shoes and overalls. Jimmy had a mama who drank. He sometimes came to school with no lunch pail and I'd share what I had. Roland didn't have a daddy. But we didn't talk about those things, just about trading marbles and stuff I barely remember now.

Lymon steps in front of me, stopping me short.

"We're talking to you and you ain't answerin'." I hear the laughing in back of me.

"What'd you say?" I ask. And then it starts. The amen choir repeats *"What'd you say?"* in a drawl sounds nothing like me.

I take a step back and land on Errol's toes. He shoves me into Lymon.

Clem stands off to the side, watching with wide eyes. I try to go around, first one side, then the other. Finally I wait while Lymon and Erroll push and shove me back and forth. If I'm quiet, they'll get tired and move on. I feel a slap on the back of my neck and they start to move away down the block. Clem's wide eyes look back at me, staring. Not nice, but not mean either. I pick up my satchel that dropped, pull down my shirt, and head home to wait alone for Daddy.

three

AT home, I check the cabinet for something, anything, to eat, and find some crackers. Daddy brings home our dinner after work. Throws some things together in a pot he heats on our hot plate and we eat quiet while our spoons bang the tin plates. Daddy's so tired he goes right to bed after. I clean up best I can then sit up, at the table, with a lamp, doing school-work. Wash up and go to bed. Across from Daddy in my bed, I listen to his snoring. Sometimes he talks a little bit in his sleep. Calls out "Teena," his nickname for Mama, in his sleep. Laughs like he used to before she got sick. But when he gets up, his face is back to what it's been since she passed.

The sounds in our apartment come alive at night. Scratching inside the walls. I've seen rats big as possums running in the halls. At night, they sound even bigger. Nothing keeps Daddy awake and I still can't make myself get used to the loud voices down on the stoop below. "Let the Good Times Roll" playing on the radio next door. A mother trying to quiet her crying baby. Daddy's snores, so close they sound like he's breathing in my ear. The brakes of the el train screeching as it comes into the station. I used to fall asleep to the sound of crickets and owls. Sometimes they were so loud I'd cover my head with my pillow. Mama and Daddy stayed awake after I was in bed, whispering, laughing softly. Sometimes I could even hear kissing and other things too. I thought I knew what loud was until I came to Chicago.

I dream of Mama too, only not at night. During the day is when I think of her. Most of the boys I knew had a houseful of brothers and sisters. Wasn't no one growing up an only like me. I never told no one, but I loved being alone with Mama. Wouldn't want it no other way. Heard womenfolk whisper once in church how it was "sad" Teena couldn't have no more children after me. But Mama made it seem like I was all she ever wanted. Like I filled her up. Like any more would have been too much. She fussed after me. Sometimes, when she was tired, she said I worked her nerves, but there wasn't nothing to it. Time I'd go out and come back again, her face lit up like I was a soldier home on leave. She never worried about me being a "mama's boy" like some folks said. She loved me hard as she could till she left this world.

Streetlights shine through the window in the front of the room. In Alabama only lights I saw at night were the moon and stars. Sometimes so bright a curtain couldn't block them out. I fall asleep most nights listening to Daddy snoring, but wishing for the sounds of an Alabama night.

There's a letter waiting today when I get home from school, sticking out of mail slot 4D. It has my daddy's name written in big, wiggly letters on the front of the envelope. I hold it up trying to see the words but can't. I'll have to wait for Daddy to get home and open it.

Upstairs the apartment is hot and stuffy even with the windows open. I lie down on my bed and it creaks as I turn on my side to face the wall. I pick at the yellowed pages of the *Chicago Defender* papering over the wall. I close my eyes and try to picture Mama. I can still see her smile with the space between her teeth. Smooth brown skin and eyes that laughed along with her. Before I know it, the tears start and won't stop. Can't believe how much I want to hear her just say my name or kiss my cheek at night. Just feel her hand rub my head like she did at night when she thought I was asleep. Sometimes I don't want to remember because with the remembering comes the hurting. I can let the water go when Daddy's not home. But when he is, I pinch myself to stop thinking about home and Mama and how my heart is missing her so much it aches. I gotta pinch myself so hard, I left a mark once. Only thing worse than crying in front of Daddy is hearing Daddy fuss when I do.

I sit up when I hear Daddy's key in the door. He comes in holding a grocery sack in his hand.

"What you doing in bed?" he asks.

"Nothing sir, t-t-t-tired is all," I stutter. Hoping my eyes ain't so puffy.

"You ain't sick, is you?" he asks. Can't tell if he's worried or mad.

"No sir, I ain't sick."

He moves to me and his rough hand reaches out. I jump back but he's just reaching to touch my forehead.

"Ain't no fever," he says, and sets down the groceries on the table. While Daddy heats up supper, I sit on my bed looking over schoolwork. The pot of beans bubbles. Daddy sets out two plates, two spoons, and a loaf of bread. Back home, Daddy never cooked a meal.

We both got up every morning to a hot breakfast of eggs and grits and sausage. The smell of it would wake me up before Daddy even called for me to get a move on. Mama packed my lunch pail for school, Daddy's for the field. She'd stand over us and watch us eat.

"Look at my hungry boys." She'd smile as we scraped up sausage, grits, and eggs. Since we left Alabama, we eat oatmeal for breakfast with a piece of toast Daddy can't help from burning.

"How's school?" Daddy asks.

I look up surprised. He never asks about school.

"Fine," I answer.

We take a few more bites in silence. "Teacher says I'm real good at my spelling words. Best in the class."

"Mmm-hmmm," Daddy answers. I can tell he's done talking.

I clear our plates, put them in the sink.

I turn on the faucet to sputtering cold water. "No hot water," I say to Daddy.

"Leave 'em be for now," he says. "I'll get 'em in the mornin'."

I go to the table, turn on the lamp, and start my schoolwork.

I see the letter, sitting on top of my books.

"Daddy, I forgot. This came today," I say, handing him the letter.

He takes his time looking at the writing. Turns it over in his hands.

"Who's it from?" I ask, wishing he'd hurry up and open it.

He turns and goes to sit on the bed. Still not opening the letter.

"Daddy?" I ask. I go to the bed.

"I'll look at it in the morning," he says. "Too tired to read right now."

"Want me to read it to you?"

He stands then. His voice is low and mad. "You think I can't read?"

"No, Daddy. It's just if you're tired is all—"

"I said I'll read it in the morning. Now go get to your schoolwork!"

He leaves the letter on the bed, grabs his towel from the hook by the bed, and heads down the hall to the bathroom.

four

THE rain started right after lunch, and I was hoping I'd get to go on home without seeing Lymon and his crew after school. But from the classroom window I can see them still waiting in the school yard. The three of them are standing around a boy, laughing. Lymon slaps the boy's lunch pail to the ground. They are keeping themselves busy till I come down. Everyone else has gone from the classroom, but I'm pretending to look for pencils in my desk.

"Can you help me carry these to my car?" Miss Robins asks, tying a rain scarf on her head.

I nearly fall rushing to help her. Parking lot is on the other side of the school yard.

"Thanks, hon," she says when I load the box into the backseat of her Buick. I shut the door.

"Bye, Mrs. Robins." I wave and walk quickly through puddles to the fence where there is an opening, looking behind to make sure no one is following. I walk fast, turning right, right again, then left onto Michigan Avenue, and keep walking till

I'm out of breath. My socks are soaked through, and by the time I stop, nothing looks familiar. Scared sweat prickles my skin. This neighborhood is quiet. The streets are wider, with tall elm trees like back home running along the sidewalks, their branches stretching over me like umbrellas.

Daddy walked me to school the first day. Pointed to the streets I would pass: "Forty-Fifth, Forty-Sixth, Forty-Seventh...just stay on this street and count up when you going to school and down when you coming home and you'll be all right," he said.

But this street looks nothing like my neighborhood. No stores and cart men. Just row after row of nice-looking houses with trees standing at the edges of sidewalks. Almost each one has swept stoops and windows with curtains that don't have signs that say FURNISHED APARTMENTS FOR RENT.

Standing on the corner across the street is a big, white stone building with another building in the middle with a pointy top. Looks like a fancy building, but I'm thinking maybe someone there can point me to Wabash. I walk closer, and carved above the door is GEORGE CLEVELAND HALL BRANCH, CHICAGO PUBLIC LIBRARY.

Once, when Daddy let me go into town with him one Saturday to get supplies for our planting, we passed a building with a sign above the door that said LIBRARY. I was just learning my letters and figured I knew just about every word ever invented, but that word I'd never seen. Daddy told me the word but said it was a building for white folks, and that meant I couldn't go in. Didn't look like nothing to me but a small little house, painted bright white, two windows in front. Other than that, I would have passed on by not noticing. But back home, in the kitchen, I asked Mama if she knew anything about a library.

"Library is a place you borrow books," Mama said, sweeping the dirt out the kitchen door.

"What kind of books?" I asked, following behind her.

"Any kind you want—books with stories and pictures 'bout anything you can think of, I reckon."

I remember thinking, *A house just for books?* "You ever been inside a library?" I asked.

She laughed then. "They don't let colored folks in libraries, baby. Now go fetch some eggs for your mama so I can start this cornbread."

While I went to the coop to fetch the eggs I thought to myself, *Any kind of books you want?*

I slowly walk up the steps to the big wooden door. A man brushes past, his arms filled with books, and I hold open the door and follow him inside. I stare up into a ceiling so big and bright, seems like God himself is looking down.

"Can I help you, young man?" a woman asks.

I can't find a way to make my mouth ask for directions to Wabash Street, so I nod and walk along behind her into sunlit silence and shelves and shelves of books. I don't see any white folks, just all kinds of colored people, some rushing past bringing books in, some bringing books out, some working at the front desk. Every one of them look like they belong here. Back home, I read all the books in my class at school till I knew them by heart. Mama said once, "They can't make books fast enough to keep up with your readin'."

Only time I ever heard Mama and Daddy fuss was about me.

"The boy's up under you too much."

Daddy said I wasted too much time reading, when I should be outside playing and helping him 'round the house.

"Henry, let the boy be. Ain't nothing wrong with him spending time with his mama."

"Sitting in the house reading ain't gonna help him grow into a man, Teena. There's things a boy's gotta learn."

"Reading is learning, Henry," Mama said, mad.

"That ain't the kind of learning I'm talking about."

Seems Mama got tired of fighting after a while. So when I wasn't in school, Daddy kept me busy working 'longside him chopping firewood, clearing brush, fixing things 'round the house needed fixing. Working and sweating side by side, Daddy didn't say it, but I could feel his pride in me then.

I walk behind the library lady. Floors look like someone just finished polishing them. So shiny, I bet if I leaned down it'd be like looking in a mirror.

"Can I help you find a book?" she says, still walking but

looking back at me. I want to say no, ask for directions to get on home, but I don't want to leave this quiet place. Again, my head nods, *yes*.

The lady starts walking farther into the library and I keep following and let myself breathe in the library smells. Old paper, glue, and wood. Smells better than Mama's peach cobbler. Everything in here is so new it makes my worn shoes look more worn. Looks like they could fit five of those little libraries from back home into this one room.

I scuff downstairs and into a smaller room with round tables and shorter bookshelves. I walk over and run my hand along the bookcases, forgetting all about asking the way home.

"Can I read one?" My voice sounds squeaky as a girl's.

"You can borrow any kind of book you want," she says kindly. "Just see the librarian at the desk."

"Any kind of book you want," I whisper to myself, and I take a few down from the shelf and pull a chair up to a table.

I trace the letters on the covers of each and stop. One has my name. I pull it out and open to the first page.

> *I pick up my life*
> *And take it with me*
> *And I put it down in*
> *Chicago, Detroit,*
> *Buffalo, Scranton.*

Feels like reading words from my heart. I keep reading till I feel a tap on my shoulder. I can tell by the sun outside, the rain stopped and it got late and that means Daddy's already home and waiting.

"We're closing soon so you'll need to make your selections," the library lady says. I tell her I got a little lost on the way over, and she shows me to the door and points.

"Walk down two blocks," she says, "then turn left on Wabash and you should be close to home."

"Thank you, ma'am."

"Hurry on home, now," she says. "I'm sure your mama will be waiting." My stomach tightens into a ball, but I run out the door and down the steps toward home.

five

I open the door.

"Why you so late?" Daddy asks, his words sharp enough to cut.

"I was out playing with some boys after school."

"Well, go wash up for supper," he says. His words are still sharp, but his eyes have a softness I haven't seen since he sat helpless as a baby by Mama's bedside.

I keep my hands under the cold water spout. Why didn't I tell Daddy about the library? Why didn't I tell him about the boys at school and the way they poke fun every day? Why didn't I tell him how alone I feel in a city full of people? Same reason I don't tell him how much I miss Mama. Don't seem like Daddy can take any more than he already got. Before we left Alabama, I heard him talking to Grandma.

"Ain't nothing left for me here, Ma."

"Leave the boy," Grandma said. "Ain't no sense in dragging him 'long till you're settled."

"She wouldn't want that," Daddy grunted. You knew when Daddy was finished talking.

I was hoping right up till we got on the train that Grandma would come with us. But saying goodbye to Alabama meant saying goodbye to everyone, even Grandma.

After we buried Mama, Daddy started selling off what little we had—the bureau, Mama's trunk. Then he started packing. Most of my things I had to leave behind.

"Take just what you need," Daddy said.

Grandma watched us go from the front porch. She squeezed me so tight, I thought she'd never let me go. All of a sudden she looked old and tired, not the Grandma who worked from sunup till sundown. Mama's death had taken something from her too. Grandma always said I had the best of my mama, and now I was leaving. Barely had a chance to talk to Jimmy and Roland. My Sunday pants rode up above my ankles while we walked the miles to the train depot. Mama never got to let them down before she passed. She said I must have grown three inches in one month, and she just couldn't keep up. Fast as she took out a hem, I grew some more. I stared hard at everything we passed so I could take a picture in my head to remember in case we never came back to Alabama. I dragged my suitcase behind Daddy's long steps. Every time Daddy slowed to take out his handkerchief and wipe his forehead, I hoped he was gonna turn around and head on home. But he just kept walking. And I just kept following. Folks stopped, asked if we wanted a ride, asked if we was heading out of town. Daddy answered, "We're just fine now. Have a good day," and kept on walking. Time we reached the depot, our clothes were soaked through.

Everyone always said I looked just like my daddy. Thick arms and middle. Big, flat feet. "Strong boy," "Handsome just like his daddy," folks been saying since the day I was born, but I never took a liking to the work Daddy did in the fields. Or chopping firewood or toting heavy bundles. That day I must have looked like his shadow trying to keep up behind his fast walking. The pebbles from the holes in the bottom of my shoes pinched every step, but I didn't slow. Figured Daddy was so mad about Mama dying, he'd leave me behind too.

Here now with Daddy that seems like such a long time ago, but I'm glad I took the pictures of Alabama in my head. They're fading, like the pictures of Mama, but they're still with me. Daddy calls from down the hall and I dry my hands on my pants and head in to supper.

At school the next day, Miss Robins is barely finished with our lesson when I start watching the clock. Fridays seem like the longest days, counting every minute till the school bell rings at the end of the day. The bell rings at 3:00, but at two minutes before, I slip my books quietly into my satchel.

BRRRRIIIINNNNG

"Okay, class, tomorrow, don't forget..."

I miss the last of what Mrs. Robins is saying as I rush toward the door. Halfway down the hall I hear "Wait for us, country boy!" so I run faster. Down the two flights of stairs, out back to the parking lot. I hide between the cars and squeeze through the hole in the fence. I don't slow down till I get to Michigan Avenue. The air feels cleaner here. Still and fresh. I turn around and there's nothing behind me but sidewalk. I cross the street and walk up the steps of the library.

six

THE library looks different today. The smooth, polished floor feels cool through the holes in my shoes. And up above, where I thought I saw God, is actually a pretty ceiling that comes to a point like a hat. I walk in circles staring up at that ceiling and bump into a woman with books.

"Excuse me ma'am," I mumble as she cuts her eyes at me.

The light comes from the tall rounded windows behind the front desk where some women stand, dressed nice and stamping books and answering questions. I don't remember how to get to the room downstairs—the room I was in yesterday, with tables and shorter bookcases. I turn one way and then another. Finally, I walk over to the front desk.

I wait, but no one says anything so I wait some more.

"I see you found your way home and back again," I hear behind me.

I turn. It's the lady from yesterday.

"Would you like to look at more books?" she asks. Wish I could make my mouth do some talking, but I mumble, "Yes ma'am."

I look close as we pass by shelves of books and big wooden tables and people sitting in chairs with round backs. We pass rows of pictures of colored people in frames like the ones in Miss Fulton's apartment. Lined up nice in one straight line. Each person smiling back, with a gold nameplate under their picture.

"Who are they?" I point at the pictures on the wall.

"They are several of the authors from our lecture series. Of course, Chicago is home to many esteemed Negro writers." She smiles. I nod like I know exactly what she's talking about.

I don't see a white person anywhere. "This a library for colored folks?" I whisper.

She stops and the smile is gone from her face. "A library for colored folks? It's a library for Chicago residents," she says, serious.

I don't know what *residents* means. But sounds to me like that means it's a colored library. We keep on walking.

"It is named for a colored man, however." She keeps walking. She has a way of talking sounds like her lips are too tight for her face. "George Cleveland Hall was a local physician. He served on the board of directors as one of the Chicago Public Library's first Negro members."

"So he built this here library?" I ask, nearly out of breath trying to keep up with her, listen about Mr. Hall, and look at the books at the same time.

She stops short and I almost walk right into her back. "He didn't build the library." She looks serious again. "But it was because of his efforts to ensure this community had a library that this branch was built fifteen years ago. It was named in his honor."

I nod again, pretending I understand. History ain't one of my favorite subjects, but I ain't ever learned any history about colored folks being physicians and directors.

Downstairs I see kids my age, some younger ones too with their mothers, sitting at smaller tables, looking though books.

When we get downstairs she says, "My name is Mrs. Kimble. I am the adult librarian, but Miss Cook at the desk will help you with your selections." Her voice is so crisp and clear, she makes every word sound special. "Miss Cook is the children's librarian."

Librarian, selections. I don't know what any of those words mean. But I aim to find out.

"Thank you ma'am."

"Mrs. Kimble," she says.

"Thank you, Mrs. Kimble," I say, happy when she turns to go back upstairs.

I go back to the shelf and back to the book with the words from my heart. I take it from the shelf, looking around to make sure it's okay. I sit at one of the empty tables close to the window and open the book.

> *I'm gonna write me some music about*
> *Daybreak in Alabama*
> *And I'm gonna put the purtiest songs in it*
> *Rising out of the ground like a swamp mist*

And falling out of heaven like soft dew.
I'm gonna put some tall tall trees in it
And the scent of pine needles
And the smell of red clay after rain.

I have to stop. I can feel the choking in my throat that always starts right before the tears. I look to make sure no one's watching, but everyone is looking at their own books. Miss Cook is at her desk, busy sorting through cards. I stand so fast I knock over my chair. Miss Cook looks up.

"Would you like to check that out?" she asks.

Check out. More words I'll need to learn.

"Ma'am?" I say.

She waves me over.

I stand in front of her at the desk and she tells me I can borrow any book I want with a library card. But first she needs my name and address.

A place where you can borrow books, I remember Mama telling me.

Before I give her my address I ask, "Are you a librarian?"

"Yes I am," she answers with a smile.

A librarian is someone who lets you borrow books in a library. One word down, I think.

"Forty-five-oh-one Wabash."

She writes that down. "And your name?"

"Langston," I tell her.

seven

LANGSTON? Any chance your last name is Hughes?"
She laughs.

I don't get the joke. She points to the book in my hand.
"Are you named after the poet Langston Hughes?"

"No ma'am. Just a name my mama and daddy picked
out, I guess."

"Well, he is a great namesake." She stamps a card and puts
it in the back of the book, then hands me a card inside a small
yellow envelope. "This is your library card. Take good care of
it, because it allows you to come back and check out books.
This is due back in two weeks."

"Two weeks? I can keep this book for two weeks?" I ask.

"Yes, then it needs to be returned."

I don't care now 'bout how many questions I ask. There's
things I need to know.

"Then I can take out more?"

"Of course. In fact you can take out up to five books at a time."

"Five?"

I sound like a parrot, repeating everything she says.

"Would you like to make more selections?"

"No ma'am," I say.

For now I just need this one here filled with pretty words.

This lady said the Langston who wrote these words is a poet. Seems more like a magician to me, pulling words from my heart I never knew I had.

"I'll be back!" I nearly shout.

She laughs again. "I'm sure you will," she says.

I walk fast as I can to get home 'fore Daddy and 'fore his questions. But I got questions of my own. I'm thinking so much about Langston Hughes, I get to my apartment before I know it.

Daddy's not home yet, and for the first time I'm happy to be alone, with my book. I lie down on my bedspread and open it slowly just as I hear Daddy's key in the door.

I squeeze the book 'tween the bed frame and the wall till it wedges in tight, then I jump up quick.

"What you doing?" Daddy asks, looking at me funny.

"Nothing sir, just thinking is all."

"Well, think over here and help me get these groceries put away," Daddy says. Fridays Daddy picks up some of our food shopping at the market on the corner. We got an account there when we moved here. The owner, Mr. Fields, is mean as can be, but Daddy says he's honest with his books, don't charge more than he has to, and that's good enough for him.

"Yes sir."

Tonight while we're eating the chicken cooked too long and rice not cooked enough, I'm missing Mama's neckbones, gravy, and cornbread bad.

Maybe that's what makes me ask him, "Why'd you and Mama name me Langston?"

"Wasn't me named you," Daddy says, his mouth full. "That name's all your mama."

"Why'd she name me Langston?"

"S'pose she liked it. She told me one day, 'We have a boy, I wanna name him Langston,' and that was that."

"You like the name?" I ask, looking down into my plate.

"Like it enough," Daddy says. "Wish you could have been named after me. Henry Junior."

I laugh then, but Daddy doesn't laugh back.

We eat the rest of our meal in silence.

Later in bed when I hear Daddy's snores I squeeze my hand next to the bed and get the book. The light coming through the front window is enough so I can just barely read the words. I turn the pages slow so Daddy can't hear. He rolls over and I quickly hide the book under my bedcovers. When the snoring starts again, I take it out. Know I should be sleeping. Know I'm going to be tired tomorrow when Daddy wakes me up. But the words make me turn page after page after page.

eight

I wake up to Daddy fussing. "C'mon, son, we gotta get a move on."

Just like back at home, Saturday is the day me and Daddy run errands. When I roll over on top of my book I look, but Daddy's back is turned to me, buttoning his suspenders. I tuck the book away and pull on my clothes.

I eat my burned toast and Daddy gathers up some papers and folds them into his jacket. Out in the hallway, loud music is coming from the apartment next door. Down two flights our neighbor on the second floor has her apartment door open and the smell of eggs and bacon frying in the skillet on the stove makes my stomach growl. We step around younger boys playing marbles on the sidewalk. Makes me wish my Saturdays were my own with nothing on my mind but friends and marbles. We start off down Wabash, cut through the alley and walk behind the buildings, over to Indiana. Out on the sidewalks in front I can pretend Chicago ain't so bad, but in the alleys and around in back of the buildings, ain't no hiding the dirt. We got to jump over puddles of dirty water and busted-up furniture, piles of trash. I hate walking in back of the buildings but it's a shortcut. Back home, we couldn't see a neighbor for miles. I'll never get used to people living on top of each other. I'll never get used to everybody knowing what time you get up in the morning and what you're cooking for breakfast. And everyone too busy to say a decent "Mornin'" when you see them on the street. Back home I had space to breathe. Had to walk down the road a ways to get to our nearest neighbor, but if somebody got sick, or was in need of a hand, folks were there to help 'fore you knew it. I knew I had to act right, because someone was always watching, waiting to get word back to my folks. Here, in a city filled with people, I can count on one hand how many know my name.

First we go to the bank so Daddy can cash his check. Then he drops off the rent money. Then Daddy tucks some bills into an envelope he mails at the post office. It's the money he mails to Aunt Lena back home. She's all alone with her three girls plus she's watching out for Grandma too. I asked Daddy once why he sends money every week when sometimes it means we gotta go without.

"A man takes care of his family," is what he said. But I thought, *Ain't I family?*

I don't mind being outside running errands, even with the days getting colder. Can't stand being cramped inside with nowhere to turn and missing Mama hanging between me and

Daddy. Makes our small apartment feel like a closet. Plus, I know when we get back to our apartment Daddy will fill the small sink with water and soap powder to wash our clothes. The sink in the corner of our room is hardly big enough to wash our dishes so it sure ain't fit for washing clothes. They never get as clean as Mama could get them with her washtub. Daddy hangs a rope across the room to hang the clothes till they dry, stiff and hard. No matter how hard Daddy wrings them, they still drip on the floor. We just gotta shake them smooth, 'cause we don't have an iron.

Saturday was always Mama's wash day. She'd sort all the clothes into piles and start to washing early in the morning before cooking breakfast. Once we got up, she stripped the sheets from the beds and washed them too. It would take near the whole day to wash, hang the clothes out on the line, and iron them, but I loved the way the house smelled clean with wood polish and soap. And on Saturday night, after my bath, when I lay in my bed, my pillowcase, worn thin from washing and sun, smelled sweet.

Our last stop is the fish market. Line is out the door, but we line up too, making our way to the counter and leaving footprints in the sawdust on the floor. Daddy likes to have fish on Saturdays, like Mama fried up back home. Fresh porgies, dipped in egg, a little cornmeal and flour, and fried in a big pot of hot grease till they were golden brown and crispy on the edges. Time Daddy finished eating, nothing but a pile of bones left on his plate. Mama would boil vinegar on the stove later to get rid of the fish smell, but Daddy don't bother about the smell in our apartment. And his fish don't taste nothing like Mama's, but I eat it just the same. Mama used to smile as she watched the bones pile up on our plates. She'd rub Daddy's back as she sat at the table, talking nonstop when our mouths were full and keeping an eye out to make sure we had enough. Tasted so good, I didn't stop eating till I felt sick.

"Next!" fish man calls out, and Daddy steps forward.

"Pound of porgies," Daddy says, "head and tails on."

"Country...," someone snickers from behind. I think it's one of the kids from school till I turn and see only grown-ups in line behind us. I look at Daddy. Don't think he heard, because he doesn't say anything and doesn't turn around. The fish man hands him the fish wrapped in brown paper.

Out on the sidewalk I say, "Ever make you mad when people call you country?"

"Ain't no shame in being from the country," Daddy says, not slowing down.

"At school...," I start. But I can't say it.

"At school what?" Daddy asks.

"Nothing," I answer.

We're just about at the fourth floor when I see Ms. Fulton coming out of her apartment with her shopping cart, and my chest gets tight. I'm so tired from staying up last night reading, I just want to get into bed and close my eyes.

"Afternoon, Miss Fulton," Daddy says.

"Afternoon, Henry," she says back, sweet as can be.

I ain't seen Daddy smile this hard since we moved to Chicago.

"Langston be happy to help you with your cart."

Langston would not be happy to help with your cart. Langston is tired and…

"That's so kind." Her smile at me ain't nothing like the one she had for Daddy. So it's back downstairs, to the market and back again, her wide behind swinging in my face all the way up the stairs with me dragging a heavy cart step by step.

Time I get back the clothes are hanging from the line and Daddy's already started frying the fish. I close the door soft and make my way to the bed when he says, "We need to get this floor swept and mopped."

I get the broom from the closet and start sweeping. As the pile of dirt grows bigger, I keep thinking, *I'm never going to stay up late reading again.*

But when the fish is gone, the plates are washed, the floor is swept and mopped, and Daddy is snoring, all I can think of is how much I wish I were back in Alabama in a house that didn't smell like fish and sound like a honky-tonk on a Saturday night, and how I wish I could hear the night sounds of crickets and feel my Mama's soft lips on my forehead. My eyes are heavy, but I still pull out the book from my hiding spot and read.

Folks, I come up North
Cause they told me de North was fine.
I come up North
Cause they told me de North was fine.
Been up here six months—
I'm about to lose my mind.

I'm not the only Langston was lied to.

Every Sunday morning we walk down the block to church. Not like the church at home, painted white with pews inside. This church got a sign painted out front says PRAISE TABER-NACLE. Daddy and I sit all the way at the back of the church that don't feel nothing like a church. More like a store, but the folks inside are dressed like church folks. And praising like church folks, jumping from their seats when the music gets good and the preacher gets to preaching loud. With hats so tall I can barely see up front. But I can hear the preacher shouting from the stage. Daddy brought along his Bible, so we read Proverbs 3:5 along with the deacon's scripture reading:

Trust in the Lord with all thine heart;
and lean not unto thine own understanding.
In all thy ways acknowledge him, and he shall direct thy
paths.

Daddy used to read his Bible every night after supper. Since Mama died, only time he picks it up is Sundays when he head to church. Got a feeling we're here 'cause he feels Mama would have wanted it for me. But his heart ain't here and neither is mine. It's like our faith got buried right along with Mama and now it's covered over with dirt and a tombstone back in Alabama.

nine

I found the letter came in the mail last week. Daddy been hiding it under his bed. I'm up late for school and Daddy left me behind. Usually we walk together to the end of the block, then he goes left for the el and I go right for school. Today I turn the apartment upside down looking for my key. I find four pennies fell out of Daddy's pocket, and one of my old marbles I been looking for. In a crack between the floorboards I finally find the key. But while I'm looking under Daddy's bed, I see a shoebox pushed all the way into the corner. I know it isn't right. Can hear Daddy's voice in my head saying looking at something don't belong to you is same as stealing. *A sin.* Folks always say my daddy is a godly man, but he don't leave much room for things that ain't a sin.

So even though I know it's a sin, I open the box and take a look. I see a couple of letters with the wiggly writing. And other letters at the bottom tied with a ribbon. These don't have envelopes, just girly writing, smell like perfume. I'll get to those later, but first I open the letter I want.

Dearest Henry,

God's blessings on you and Langston hope you both are well in chicago bet it's cold there now. Henry I'm sorry to tell you mama is doing poorly. Since she got that cold last month she just can't seem to get right. Keep me up half the night coughing not that I'm complaining God has blessed me with the strength to carry on in good times and bad. We sure appreciate the money you been sending but with her cough getting worse I may need a little something extra to get her to the doctor if you have it to spare.
Tell Langston be good for his daddy.

prayerfully yours,
Lena

Grandma is sick? I never seen my grandma sick a day in my life. I barely saw Grandma sit down, let alone take to bed. Mama said that was because she was used to taking care of herself after Daddy's daddy died. Since then, she had to be a mama and a daddy. A man and a woman I guess. She cooked just as good as she farmed. Sundays after services, seemed like half the church would come by for supper. Grandma had a long table and she'd lay out dish after dish on her old lace tablecloth. After the ham, macaroni and cheese, fried okra, biscuits, green beans swimming in butter, and sweet tea, Mama and Aunt

Lena cleared the table and brought out the pies. Grandma sat at the head telling stories.

When Mama took sick, was Grandma came and tended to her when me and Daddy couldn't. Treated Mama like a newborn baby. Washing her, feeding her, changing the sheets when she wet herself. And at night, after Grandma cooked our dinner and cleaned up too, she sat by the bed, brushing and plaiting Mama's hair, and singing songs so sweet my eyes filled with water. She loved Mama near as much as me and Daddy.

"God blessed me with another child I didn't have to birth or burp," she'd say, and laugh. She knew Mama's family 'fore Mama was even born. Her people lived down the road till they passed when Mama was still young.

I am so late now, I'm gonna get sent to the office. I put the key in my shoe and race down the steps to school.

The principal, Mr. Freeman, is talking to a teacher when I run into the office for a late pass, and he just waves me on to class. I slip into my seat, trying to quiet my breathing so Mrs. Robins don't turn around from the chalkboard.

Between the letter and being late, I barely notice that Lymon didn't come to school. Means I can take my time going to the library. Clem and Erroll barely look at me as I walk through the school yard. On the way to the library I notice the trees in the sidewalk have leaves that are just starting to turn yellow. The same yellow I watched from my bedroom back home every year when the weather started to turn.

In the spring the smell of white blossoms made Mama smile, and on a hot Alabama day you could almost hide from the sun under its branches. Every year, when the first flowers showed up, Mama would cut off a few branches and put them in water in a mason jar. Sit them right in the middle of the kitchen table.

"So we don't have to go outside to smell springtime," she'd laugh. Daddy said she was looking at too many of those white women's magazines, but I thought they looked real pretty. Think he did too. We both loved how white blossoms on a branch could make her so happy.

Downstairs in the library I plop my book on the librarian's desk.

"Finished early. I want to take out more," I tell her.

She laughs. "That's fine. Here…" She points. "The return slot is there. Just put them in there and go check out more books."

"Thanks," I mumble, 'shamed again to not know yet how the library works.

"You have any books on trees?" I ask.

"Right over there in the nonfiction section. Try the 580 call numbers," she says.

Don't know what *nonfiction* means or if there are really 580 books on trees, but I look anyhow.

I walk up and down the rows and then I see one book and a lot more all about trees. All kind of trees too. I never knew there were so many. I take one of the tree books down from the shelf and go to the table by the window. I look through the pictures for a magnolia tree and find one, right in the middle of the book. A big color picture, smooth and shiny. I add another Langston Hughes book on top of the magnolia book and pull my card out of my satchel and wait for the librarian to thunk a stamp in my books.

ten

I'M *in Alabama, under the shade of a magnolia with red ants crawling up my trouser legs and the buzz of gnats swarming my head. The sun is hot but under the branches it feels almost cool. Mama sits on the porch fanning away flies. She laughs when she sees me and—*

"Langston?" I look up at Mrs. Robins' bony knees.

"Langston, the bell rang five minutes ago," she says. "Time to come inside."

"Sorry, ma'am, I didn't hear it," I mumble.

"Well, if you put down that book you might," she says, sharp. "What are you reading, anyway?" she asks, walking ahead into the school.

"I found a book in the library about magnolia trees, just like the ones back home in—"

"It's time to focus on school now, Langston, and not trees. And you're not in the South anymore. You're a smart boy, but you need to focus on doing well here in Chicago."

"Yes ma'am," I say.

We can hear the classroom from down the hall. Without Mrs. Robins in the room, they're loud and horsing around. When I walk in, it gets quiet. I walk to my seat.

"Happened to you, country boy?" the boy in the desk behind me asks.

"Scared to come back in, I guess," laughs Lymon.

"*Quiet, class!*" Mrs. Robins yells. "Time to get back to work. Let's get our history textbooks opened to page 65, please."

At the end of the day I'm walking my usual fast leaving the school, pushing past all the kids in the school yard, and I just about make it to the fence when I see him. He's right there at the sidewalk waiting. Ain't going to be no getting home in a hurry now to read 'fore Daddy gets home. Spent all this time hating being alone, and now all I want is the quiet to look at my books. Plus, I got a box of letters under Daddy's bed needs looking at. But Lymon ain't interested in letters and books. Lymon is interested in Langston. So when he starts his stuff, I tell him, "*Leave me alone!*" Yell it right in his face. Lymon is so shocked he don't say nothing at first. That is, till Errol and Clem start laughing.

"He told you, Lymon," they chant.

When he sees me sorta smiling and trying to keep walking, his fist hits my mouth so hard, I near think my head will break in two.

"*Fight! Fight!*" I hear everyone yelling. This ain't what I want, but Lymon's wound up. Before he swings again, one of the teachers who's supposed to be watching us yells, "*Enough!*"

Red-faced, he stands with his hands on his hips. Looks like he's ready to snatch us both up. "*Go on home now,*" he shouts to the crowd as everyone begins walking away.

Lymon leans over, whispers in my ear: "See you tomorrow, country boy."

Time I get to Wabash I've wiped most of the blood from my lip. But I can feel it getting big and know Daddy's gonna be mad. Daddy's always wanting me to turn the other cheek till I ain't got another cheek to turn.

I'm digging the key out of my shoe when I hear Miss Fulton's door open behind me. I pretend I don't hear.

"Langston," she says.

She does know my name.

"Ma'am," I say, not wanting to turn till I can wash off my lip.

"You hear me talking to you?" she asks.

"Yes ma'am," I say, still not turning, still digging for my key.

She walks over and pulls at my shoulder.

"When I'm talking to you, I—" she stops. "What happened to your lip?" she asks.

"Oh, nothing, ma'am. Just horsing 'round with some boys at school." Don't like lying, but there ain't no way I'm talking to her about much of anything.

"You're going to need to put something on that," she says. "Come with me."

I follow her into her apartment. "Sit there," she says, and points to a chair.

She goes to the sink. First she dabs at my lip with a wet cloth. Then she pours a little something from a bottle on the shelf and dabs that on my lip.

"*Ow!*" I yell. "*Burns!*"

"Just a little, but it will keep it from getting infected."

"Thanks, Miss Fulton," I say, getting up to leave. "I gotta be getting home now. 'Fore Daddy gets in."

She stares at me. Head tilted to the side like she's trying to decide something serious.

"Well, okay then," she says finally.

In the apartment, I go to the table and take out the tree book. But now I can't see Mama on the porch or the ants crawling up my legs. Just see Lymon and hear Errol and Clem laughing. Tomorrow's going to be worse than today. I close the book and take out my schoolbooks. I can hear the slow thump of Daddy's feet up the steps. Then I hear Miss Fulton's door open across the hall and Daddy's steps stop. I can hear them talking, but not so good. I get up and listen closer at the door. They talk so long I go back to the table and my books. Finally I hear Daddy's key in the door.

"Hi, Daddy," I say, head in my books, not looking up.

"Son," he says. He puts a greasy sack on the table. "Picked up chicken from the place on the corner."

I stand to get the plates but Daddy grabs my shoulder. Turns my head to him.

"What happened?" he asks, looking at my lip.

I'm tired. And my lip is hurting. And I hate Lymon. And the tree book ain't good to me no more. And I miss my mama. But I can't say any of those things, so I just let the water go. One big drop after the next. Daddy sits me down and pulls up the other chair close.

eleven

DADDY takes a gray, linty handkerchief from his pocket.

"Wipe your eyes," he says.

I wipe but the tears keep coming. We sit quiet, looking everywhere but at each other.

Finally I say, "I want to go back to Alabama."

"Can't do that, son," Daddy says. "Our home is here now."

"This ain't my home," I say before thinking. Daddy doesn't stand for any back talk, but he sits quiet.

"Langston…" Daddy sighs. "This is our chance for something better. Alabama was my home too, but after your mama passed…" Daddy looks like he's choking, then starts again. "After your mama passed, I knew I couldn't stay. For me, Alabama is her and us. Without her, ain't nothing left for me there."

Fast as they started, my tears stop. And I can finally look up at Daddy. I hand him back his handkerchief and he dabs at his eyes hard.

"Every year me and your mama worked, seemed like we fell deeper in debt to Mr. Clanton. Getting out was the only way to get ahead. Me and your mama heard a lot of folks talk about up north, a man can provide for his family without always scraping and bowing. Your mama wanted to come north something bad. She didn't want you working a plot. We were just waiting…waiting for the right time, I guess. Then it was too late. I was lucky to get my job down at the plant. Lucky folks here still want to hire a colored man, with all the soldiers coming back. I ain't gotta spend my days yessiring and nosiring. Just do the work, and collect my check at the end of the week. With enough to help out back home too. Helps me hold my head just a little bit higher. You understand what I'm saying?"

I nod.

"We gotta make the best of this. For your mama. She'd be proud of you going to school. And me, making a way."

"But don't you miss Grandma and Aunt Lena and being back in—"

He don't let me finish. "I'm planning on sending for them soon as I can," he says. "Soon as I can get a bigger place, some more money saved."

Hearing that makes my heart beat a little bit faster, thinking about Grandma and Aunt Lena and my cousins coming to Chicago.

Daddy stands. "Let's get started on dinner 'fore it gets cold," he says.

But I ain't got no appetite, thinking about Lymon and tomorrow.

"I hear you had some trouble today at school."

Big mouth Miss Fulton.

"Wasn't nothing really," I say, pretending to eat. "Just horsing around and I slipped."

"You know lyin' is a sin," Daddy says.

"Yessir."

"Go on and tell me what happened." Daddy reaches for more chicken.

I take a deep breath. "There's a boy Lymon. He's real mean. Calls me 'country boy.'"

"Country boy?" Daddy laughs with his mouth full.

I don't see what's funny. "Lymon and his friends…"

"Friends?"

"Yeah, Errol and Clem. They always on me too. They say my overalls is country, and the way I talk. Today he punched me when I told him to leave me alone."

"Hmmm." Daddy looks like he's doing some serious thinking.

"He says tomorrow he gonna finish what he started."

"Hmmm," again from Daddy. "What you do when he hit you?" he asks.

"Kept walking," I say. Daddy's asking more questions than he's giving answers. So I ask, "What you think I should do?"

"Bible says turn the other cheek," Daddy says.

I knew that was coming, but I just nod like it's the first time I heard it.

Daddy is washing up the dishes when we hear a knock on the door. Both of us surprised, 'cuz ain't no one ever knocked on our door before.

"Who is it?" Daddy asks.

"It's Pearl, Henry."

Who is Pearl?

Daddy opens the door and Miss Fulton is standing there holding two plates. "I made some apple pie tonight and thought maybe you and Langston might like some."

"Why thank you, Pearl." *When did Daddy start calling her Pearl?* He reaches for the plates.

"Like to come in for a minute?" Daddy asks.

"Oh no, no.... I just wanted to drop those off. Figured you could both use a little something to sweeten your day."

"Thank you, Pearl. I get these plates back to you in the morning."

"No rush, Henry," Miss Fulton says. Didn't even know she could smile like that. Her teeth are so white and pretty they could light up a room.

Daddy hands the plates to me and closes the door.

We sit at the table and eat about some of the best apple pie I ever had. Me and Daddy's plates barely need washing, we scrape them so clean.

Miss Fulton was right. This day really did need some sweetening.

When me and Daddy leave for school in the morning, Daddy turns right 'stead of left to the el train.

"I'm gonna walk you to school today," Daddy says.

I barely slept last night thinking about Lymon. I thought about pretending I was sick, but seeing as I told Daddy all about yesterday, wasn't no use. Daddy's walking fast. I know his boss down at the Maxwell Brothers plant will give him a hard time if he's too late. Daddy said they fired one man came in late two days in a row. Daddy takes the el and a bus to get to work, but he still gets there early every day.

"Don't believe in giving them one more excuse to knock a colored man down," Daddy says all the time.

We walk through the school yard, still almost empty. We go right up the front stairs, turn left inside, and Daddy walks into the principal's office. He tells me to wait outside.

Time Daddy comes out, the hall has filled and emptied again.

"Go on to class," Daddy says. "I'll see you at home later."

I go on up to class late and look around the room for Lymon. He sits all the way in the back, but his chair is empty.

If Daddy got Lymon in trouble with the principal, it's gonna be worse for me than before. I sit at my desk and look like I'm listening to Mrs. Robins go on and on, just counting the minutes till three o'clock.

twelve

FIRST thing I do when I get to the library is walk row by row, seeing what books make me stop. Some of the titles I can't help but pull off the shelves. I try to take out as many as I can each time. Means my satchel is heavier than a bag of rocks, but I keep them there out of sight. It's better to read in the library. Sitting at my favorite table by the window reading and listening to the sound of other folks turning pages makes me feel like I'm in a house full of company I don't have to talk to.

Miss Cook sometimes puts aside books she thinks I'll like. 'Specially the ones by Langston Hughes. Every time she hands me one of his she says, "Here's another from your namesake." I know there ain't no chance Mama named me for a poet who wrote pretty words, but it feels good to hear her say it.

Red Clay Blues

I want to tramp in the red mud, Lawd, and
Feel the red clay round my toes.

I want to wade in that red mud,
Feel that red clay suckin' at my toes.
I want my little farm back and I
Don't care where that landlord goes.

In Langston Hughes' words I can smell that earthy clay in the front yard. Can hear the voice of my mama.

I make my way over to Miss Cook's desk.

"Excuse me, ma'am." She looks up.

"Is Mr. Langston Hughes from Alabama?"

"Good question. Let's see if we can find out." She gets up and walks me back to the nonfiction section. She pulls one book off the shelf and hands it to me.

"This is a biography by the author, so it's a good place to start."

"Biography?" I ask. "Like a story about his life?" I learned that in school.

"Yes, exactly." She smiles. "You may just find you have a lot in common with your namesake."

"I'll check this one out," I tell her.

I can see Daddy on the stoop as I get close to the apartment. He's looking for me so I pick up my pace.

"Where you been?" Daddy yells, not even waiting for me to walk up the steps. He don't wait for an answer. "Something happened and I got to go."

"Where we going?" I ask, scared.

"Not we, me. You gonna stay here."

In the apartment, Daddy's suitcase is sitting on the bed, piled with his clothes, his black suit and tie on top.

"Where you going?" I don't know when I been more scared.

Daddy sits on the bed.

"Son," he starts. "Your grandma took a turn. Your aunt Lena called at my job. She passed this mornin'."

"Grandma?" Feels like I can't breathe.

"I'm gonna come with—"

"Can't, Langston. Barely got enough for one fare, let alone two. My boss said I could take a week and settle my affairs, then I'll be back."

"But Daddy, how am I gonna—"

"Now, I talked to Pearl—Miss Fulton—and she's gonna look in on you every day. Gonna make your meals and such, and see you off to school while I'm gone."

I can't imagine this day getting any worse, but it just did. The last morning I saw Mama alive, Grandma sent me off to school.

"You're not doing anybody any good sitting 'round with that long face," she told me. "I'll look after your mama. She'd want you in school," Grandma said as she fixed me a big plate of fried eggs. But, after school, just before I got to the house, I could see saw Pastor Lawson coming down the front steps and I could see Daddy's big arm around Grandma's shoulders and

Grandma wiping her eyes with her handkerchief. I ran hard as I could. Time I got to the porch I was out of breath and I knew why the pastor was there.

"*She's gone?*" I screamed, running into the house. Mama was laid out on the bed. Grandma had brushed out her hair, put her in a clean gown.

And now Grandma. She'll never get a chance to see Chicago. I sit down to keep my head from spinning.

Daddy jumps up and snaps his suitcase shut. "Gotta leave now if I'm gonna make the train." I wrap my arms around Daddy's waist, my head in his chest. His shirt still has the sour smell from the paper plant. Probably ain't done this since I was little, but I don't care. Don't want Daddy to go and leave me alone in Chicago. Feels like I'm losing everyone.

"Can't I go too?" I sound like a baby, but I don't care.

"Already explained it, Langston. I'll be back in one week." He pulls free and heads for the door.

As I hear him go down the stairs, I sprawl on my bed. No tears, no fussing, just my head filling with pictures of my grandma.

There's a knock on the door and I don't need to guess who it is. I take my time getting up.

I open the door and Miss Fulton steps in without being invited.

"I'm so sorry about your grandmother, Langston," she says. She takes a look around the apartment. "So I guess your Daddy told you I'll be checking in on you?"

"Yes ma'am."

"Supper should be ready soon. You must have homework to do. You can get started on that, and I'll knock when it's time to eat. Would you be more comfortable sitting with me across the hall?" Miss Fulton looks nervous.

"No ma'am. I'll stay here and do my homework."

"Okay then."

Over supper, I can see Miss Fulton is trying. And I know I should be trying back. But between my daddy being gone and my grandma passing on, I can't make myself.

"How was school today?" Miss Fulton asks.

"Fine," I say.

I'll say one thing for Miss Fulton. She can put together some dinner. I ain't had a meal this good since I left home. Pork chops smothered in gravy, green beans floating in butter, cornbread hot and fluffy. I'm 'bout to burst, but I can't stop eating.

"You were hungry," she says as I scoop more gravy onto my plate to dip the rest of my cornbread.

"Yes ma'am."

I don't look up again till the cornbread is gone and my plate is clean.

thirteen

DADDY hasn't been gone one day and already I don't care much for being alone. But the one thing 'bout Daddy being gone is I can read all I want right out in the open like at the library. Feels good to see all my books unpacked and piled on the floor next to my bed. I pick up the biography and can't get past the cover for staring at his name and the title, *The Big Sea*. On the back of the book I see his picture. Brown just like me, with shiny, wavy hair like the ladies that come out of the beauty parlor on Saturdays. His smile reminds me of the pictures I saw lined in a row. The *esteemed Negro writers* Miss Kimble talked about when I first visited the library. Now I'm going to need to go and see if Mr. Hughes' picture's been hanging upstairs the whole time I been downstairs reading his books. I imagine him my age and think of all the questions I need answers to. What books did he read? How did he start writing poetry? Why did he...and all of a sudden I remember the letters.

The box is still pushed into the corner under Daddy's bed. Daddy's voice is in my head but it's not making me stop reaching for the letters in the bottom of the box. The ribbon is old and crinkly and nearly falls apart when I untie it. The ink is so faded I can't read all the words, but I see words I don't want to see, like *Henry. Love. Night. Baby. Teena.*

My head is pounding fast as my heart. Letters from Mama. Now it does feel like I'm stealing. Stealing secrets from Mama and Daddy. Secrets I ain't supposed to know. But 'stead of tying the letters up and putting them back in the box, I spread them out on Daddy's bed and just look. Mama's writing was always so neat. With big loops and little ones—*my fancy writing*, she used to call it. I always keep a piece of Mama with me wherever I go, and now I know Daddy does too, in this box under his bed. Now I took his piece too. I start folding up each letter, neat as I can, but stop when I get to the next to last one.

My black one,

Thou art not beautiful
Yet thou hast

A loveliness
Surpassing beauty.

Mama was so tired after working our plot and putting dinner together, she could barely keep her eyes open after supper. Ain't no way she sat and wrote poetry.

There's so many questions in my head I can't think. *A love-liness surpassing beauty.* Wish I could have seen what Daddy wrote back if he did. Is this what they whispered at night when I had to cover my head with my pillow?

I finish folding up the letters and tie the ribbon. Slip them back in the box and sit on Daddy's bed. Tired now but not sleepy. Gotta head over to Miss Fulton's for supper soon, so I put my books back in my satchel. All except the biography. I turn to the first page still thinking about how you could know someone so well but not know them at all.

I make myself keep moving so I'm not late again for school. Without Daddy moving fast in the morning, keeping me going till we get out the door, seems I just can't make myself move fast. Daddy told Miss Fulton I can make my own break-fast, only I wish he hadn't, because after I burned the last two pieces of bread I had to eat some crackers and a nasty, shriveled-up apple. I bet Miss Fulton makes a mean breakfast with eggs and sausage and gravy.... I run out the door zipping my jacket, trying not to think 'bout how empty my belly is.

Straight after school, I rush to the library and downstairs to tell Miss Cook that Langston Hughes isn't from Alabama but from Missouri and Kansas. On the map at school, I saw they are next-door neighbors to Illinois. That he traveled all over the world and went to college in New York and loved living there in a place called Harlem. That when he traveled the world and lived far from his mama, he was lonely too and wrote poems about it. That he ...

Clem is standing at the desk talking to Miss Cook. *They followed me here?* I look around quick for Lymon and Errol and don't see them anywhere. But that don't make no sense. Clem bothers with me only if Lymon is around. I'm standing still not knowing which way to turn when Clem looks up. Stares right at me.

"You boys know each other from school?" Miss Cook asks just as sweet as can be.

"Nope," we both say at the same time.

"Oh? Pardon me, you looked like you knew each other." She stamps the book Clem is holding.

"These are due back in two weeks, Clem," she says.

Clem walks past me with his head down. Something inside me starts growing till my chest is pounding. I follow him out and take the steps two at a time behind him. At the top, I say, "You here with Lymon and Errol?"

"Get away from me, country boy," he says, and keeps on walking.

I grab his arm to stop him. *"I ain't your country boy!"* Words coming out louder than I knew they could. Don't know when I been this mad. *"You can't be following me here!"*

"Boys," Miss Cook says from the bottom of the stairs. "Keep your voices down."

"Look, I ain't here with Lymon or Errol. Just came to get some ... some books is all."

Here in the stairwell, Clem looks so small and skinny. Me and my big self looks like I could crush him without trying hard. I let his arm go.

"This where you come after school?" Clem asks.

"Why you asking? You bringing Lymon back?"

"He don't know. . . . I come by myself some Thursdays when my mama gotta work late for her family."

My mind is working hard trying to figure if he's lying or tricking me or just likes books as much as I do. All I can get out is "Mmm-hmmm."

"You come every day?" Clem asks, like everything's okay between us when he knows it ain't.

"What's it to you?" I ask.

"You ever come when those big-time writers are here for their meetings? Once there was so many folks upstairs, Miss Kimble came downstairs to get extra chairs."

"What big-time writers?" I ask, before I remember I'm not even supposed to be talking to Clem. But I am hoping Clem knows more about the writers upstairs in the pictures.

"Ah, I don't know any of their names, but Miss Kimble said they're *famous*. That their work is *important*." The last words he says with a fancy girl's voice as he stretches his neck forward and blinks fast, then laughs.

I can't help but smile a little bit.

"See you later," Clem says. "I gotta get on home."

I wait till I see Clem leave then I walk toward the front of the library, past the tall bookshelves and toward the row of pictures. At long, wooden tables folks sit reading or with books spread out, some scribbling down words on pads of paper. At other tables folks are whispering together. I make sure no one is watching me, and then I walk to the end of the row. The first picture is a woman, the second too. That makes me stare a little longer 'cuz I never knew women wrote books, 'specially colored women. But here are their pictures on the wall and their names underneath, MARGARET WALKER and GWENDOLYN BROOKS. I keep walking down the row past RICHARD WRIGHT, ARNA BONTEMPS, and then I stop in front of Langston Hughes. I don't even need to look down at his name to recognize his face and shiny, wavy hair. Don't know how long I stand staring 'fore I hear "Excuse me" behind me. An older lady is waiting to get past and I move to the side. 'Shamed now to have been standing staring at pictures I know no one else ever stops to look at. I head on back downstairs. But now, sitting at the table with my books, I'm just pretending to read. My mind is wondering if I'll ever meet Langston Hughes at the library. And wondering too if Clem is gonna tell Lymon he saw me here.

I feel Miss Cook's hand on my back. She leans over. "Is everything okay, Langston?" she asks.

I look at her and nod, packing up my books.

Walking home, I think about me chasing after Clem and I feel lighter somehow. It's not till I get to my steps I realize it's the first time I ever yelled at someone.

fourteen

TURNS out Miss Fulton ain't no trouble at all. Almost like she took a vacation from herself. After being alone with Daddy for so long I ain't used to this much talking, but it ain't so bad. I figure her living alone makes her want to talk. Besides, her food is so good, her steady talking gives me more time to eat. And she is pretty. Prettier than I thought, at least. Her skin is smooth and her eyes light up when she's telling a story. Her hair is pulled into a bun on top of her head and she has those pearl earrings I've seen rich ladies wearing. My mama didn't even have her ears pierced. She said she wouldn't waste her money on earrings. But Miss Fulton's earrings and hair and proper talk make her look like a real lady. She teaches English at Dunbar High School. Born and raised in Chicago. Got two sisters and one brother. She talks so much, I could write her biography.

"All your folks live in Chicago?" I ask between mouthfuls, just to keep her talking so I can keep on eating.

"Funny you asked," she says, getting up from the table. She

brings over one of the pictures she keeps in a frame. "These are my parents, Anne and Elbert Fulton. They came here from the South, like you. Only from Charlottesville, Virginia. But I was born here, the oldest of four. My parents still live at Forty-Fifth and St. Lawrence."

She looks proud and keeps staring at the picture.

"So your brothers and sisters live in Chicago?" I reach for another spoonful of rice and Miss Fulton doesn't even notice.

"My brother William lives in Indiana with his family. But my sisters are here. One is at Crane College over on the West Side and the other is a teacher like me."

I nod. Sounds to me like she comes from a real smart family.

"You always wanted to be a teacher?"

"For as long as I can remember. I've always loved reading, so I didn't know what else to be. After I finished high school, I enrolled in college, just part-time at first...." Looks like Miss Fulton been waiting for me to ask this question. Her eyes are bright and she's leaning toward me in her seat.

"I had an aunt who was also a teacher and she encouraged me to get an education degree. So that's what I did, and now..." Miss Fulton acts like she doesn't remember because she starts counting on her fingers. "This will be my tenth year teaching."

"What kind of books does your class read?" Two more years before I'm in high school and I'm already counting the days till I get out of Haines Junior High and away from Lymon.

"We just started a unit on poetry," she tells me. That makes me put down my fork.

"Poetry?"

"Yes," she answers, and walks over to a small bookcase in the corner. Stacked on top are magazines she sets on the floor, some with pictures of black folks on the cover. I'd like to get a look at the ones with names like *Life*, *The Crisis*, and *Ebony*, but I'll have to ask Miss Fulton another time. Never even noticed any of this before, probably because I was too busy smelling her lavender smell.

"Of course, the school likes me to teach all the classic poets—Emerson, Frost, Dickinson—but I always include some of our own as well. Paul Laurence Dunbar for one," she says, opening one of the books she sets on the table and turning to the first page to the list of poets.

"So, all these are colored poets?" I look down the list of names I never heard of.

"Yes, they are. Many are from the Harlem Renaissance, and some"—she turns the page—"are from right here in Chicago." My head is trying to keep everything straight. *Harlem*. I know that from reading the biography.

"Harlem, New York?" I ask, but really telling because I want her to know I know a little something.

"Exactly," she says, brightening up the room again with her smile.

I go back to looking at the names. Arna Bontemps. Gwendolyn Brooks. I know these names from the library pictures. Countee Cullen. W.E.B. Du Bois. Jessie Fauset. These I don't. Right away I see Mr. Langston Hughes.

"You'll be reading Langston Hughes?" I ask.

"Oh yes. He's one of my favorites." She smiles some more. "In fact," she says, serious now, "I heard him read one of his works not too long ago at the Hall Library. They have a wonderful lecture forum run by the librarian there. Do you know his work?"

"I s'pose." I don't know how much I want to be telling Miss Fulton. Me and the library and books and Mr. Langston Hughes are something I'm keeping to myself.

"Maybe I'll read something of his after dinner," she says.

"If you want," I say, hoping she can't see how much I want to hear her read.

I help her scrape the plates, wash and dry the dishes. And then we sit at the table and Miss Fulton picks up the other book. Its pages are old and worn, some are just about to fall out, some have folded-down corners, but she finds the page she's looking for and starts reading.

The Negro Mother

Children, I come back today
To tell you a story of the long dark way . . .

I close my eyes, listening. His words sound even prettier without me stumbling over them in my head. Miss Fulton reads in a way that sounds like she's singing a song.

"Langston, are you awake?" she asks.

"Yes, Miss Fulton." I open my eyes.

"Oh . . . you looked like you were asleep." She keeps on.

I make my eyes stay open and watch her mouth sound out each word, making them sing. Finally she finishes.

I don't care what she thinks now. "Can you read that one more time?" I ask her.

"How about I read another?" she says, flipping to one of the turned-down pages.

"No, that one, please."

I think she sees something in my face that says I need to hear it again, 'cuz she doesn't ask any more questions, turns back the pages, and starts again.

When I lie in my bed that night, I think about Grandma and how I never got a chance to say goodbye. When Mama passed, Grandma told me Mama is always gonna be my guardian angel.

"She'll be looking out for you wherever you go," she said. "So don't you go shamin' her. Respect yourself and everyone round you and you'll make her proud."

I nearly cried myself to death thinking about Mama up in heaven, all alone. But now Grandma'll be with her. The both of them my guardian angels.

First night since I came to Chicago, the night sounds are quiet. No music from next door, no loud talking on the stoop, even the rats scratching in the wall are quieter. After Miss Fulton's reading, I don't want to hear my voice reading tonight. I'm just holding on to hers. But I remember the names from the pictures and in the book, and soon as I leave school tomorrow, those are the ones I'll be looking for in the library.

fifteen

WALKING to the library I zip my jacket against the wind and take my time getting there. Some of the leaves are off the trees, all colors of red and yellow and orange too. Still no Lymon in class and I'm almost invisible to Errol and Clem. Aside from Ruby, with her clothes that always look two sizes too small, who sits in back of me and can't stop talking even to me, no one has much to say.

> *Sometimes when I'm lonely,*
> *Don't know why,*
> *Keep thinkin' I won't be lonely*
> *By and by.*

Langston Hughes' poem comes into my head, drowning out her whispering that ain't really whispering 'cuz Mrs. Robins can hear her clear in front of the room.

"Ruby, I'm the only one speaking now!" Mrs. Robins screams.

And just like that, Mr. Hughes' poem disappears.

Clem doesn't even look my way since I saw him at the library, which is fine with me. One block from the library I hear fast steps behind me. I walk faster and the steps get faster too. And then I hear someone running up behind me. I spin around just as Clem is right at my back and I step to the curb and curl my hands into fists.

"Relax, country boy," Clem says, laughing.

"What you want?" I say, mad. I gotta move fast today to get my books. Miss Fulton said Daddy may be home tonight.

"Just walking to the library is all," Clem says. "Returning my books." He points to his satchel.

I relax a little then but not much.

"Thought you only came on Thursdays."

"Yeah, well, my mama had to work extra for her family. They're having a *big to-do party* tonight and you know white folks can't barely do for themselves," he says, laughing to himself. Clem thinks most of what Clem says is funny.

"So your mama keeps house?" I ask.

"Yup, for the Franklin family, live over in Hyde Park. My sisters, they're in high school, s'posed to be watching me, but they're too busy with their boyfriends. So I can do what I want long as I don't say nothing to our mama." Clem laughs again.

"Ain't seen Lymon around lately. Where's he been?"

"Why, you miss him?" His smile stretches from ear to ear. Can't see nothing but teeth when Clem smiles.

"I don't care. Just wondering is all."

"Errol said he may be going to a different school. Ain't my concern."

"Ain't he your friend?" I ask. Can't believe I'm talking this much to Clem, let alone about Lymon.

Clem shrugs and we walk side by side up another block. We must look like a sight. Me tall and thick, Clem short and skinny.

Since I'm asking so many questions, I try another. "What kind of books you read?"

Clem opens his satchel and pulls out a beat-up book with a picture of a map on the cover.

"This here's a story about a boy and his sisters. They take this boat to an island and all kinds of things happen to 'em. I already read the first, but this one's my second. Still got nine more to read." Clem talks so fast he barely takes a breath. Wish I could take back the question because I sure don't want to tell him I'm reading poetry. "One day, I'm gonna join the Navy and travel the world, just like my daddy."

Don't get a chance to ask Clem about his daddy in the Navy because he keeps on.

"The best part is when they…" I'm half listening, wondering why I'm even talking to Clem but not minding how it feels to be walking with someone, anyone, to the library after school. Thinking it may feel kinda good to talk about books. We get to the corner and cross the street to the library, head right downstairs.

"See you later," Clem says, and starts walking to the bookshelves.

"Clem," I say before he leaves. "My name is Langston."

Clem nods and I go to the desk. Miss Cook isn't here today but there is an older lady with gray hair. She barely looks up.

"Put your returns in the slot," she says.

"Ma'am?" I say. She looks up and stares through her little round glasses, saying nothing.

"Where can I find books on Frost and Gwendolyn Brooks and Countee Cullen and Dickinson?"

She sighs. "Over there with poetry in the 800 section." Now I know what the numbers mean. *Call numbers*, Miss Cook told me, and she explained how they work. She laughed when I asked how librarians can remember titles, writers, and numbers too. This woman at the desk says "*poetry*" so loud, Clem looks over. I walk fast over to poetry and I don't see any with the name Dickinson, but I do see one by Robert Frost. I take that, and they even have the book Miss Fulton read, with poems by Countee Cullen and all the other colored poets. When she showed me I made sure to remember the words on the cover—*Caroling Dusk*. I take that one too.

I wave goodbye to Clem and leave the library as fast as I can. It's cooler now as I walk home, and even though I miss the Alabama warmth, the cold makes me feel awake. I pull out *Caroling Dusk* and look through the first pages. I walk and read at the same time, trying not to fall off the curbs. Sidewalks are something I can't quite get used to, because you always got to pay attention to where you're walking. I get to my building still reading the poetry, different from Langston Hughes but with words I like. I figure there must be a world of Negro poets I don't even know yet.

At the door, I hear sounds from inside the apartment and I hurry to get my key. Daddy's home. *"Daddy!"* I yell soon as I see him. And then I see Miss Fulton sitting at the table.

Daddy smiles big like he missed me. I go to hug him hard and my book hits his side.

"What's this?" Daddy asks. I forgot all about the book in my hand.

"Something I'm reading for school," I say, my face getting hot.

Please don't let Miss Fulton see it, I say over and over in my head.

"I better be going," she says in a hurry, like she's watching something she shouldn't be. "I'll check in on you both later."

"Son, you thank Miss Fulton for all she done while I was gone," Daddy says.

I fold my arm behind my back, hiding the book. "Thanks, Miss Fulton."

"Langston was very good company," she says, smiling at Daddy.

I wait till the door closes to let all my questions spill out at once.

sixteen

EVEN though Daddy stayed up late answering every one of my questions about Grandma's services, and Aunt Lena and her kids, he left early for work this morning. I can tell being away for a whole week from a job that don't mind firing colored workers is on his mind. When I'm locking the door behind me to leave for school, Miss Fulton is coming out of her apartment.

"Morning, Miss Fulton."

"Oh, good morning, Langston," she says. "Mind if I walk with you a bit?"

Can tell it ain't a question. What else am I supposed to say but "No ma'am."

She walks next to me quiet at first and just when I get to thinking that maybe this is the one day she ran out of things to say, Miss Fulton says, "I see you got one of the books I showed you out of the library."

"It was just a book from school," I say.

"Langston." She stops and looks at me. "There is no shame

in being a reader. And being someone who loves poetry. Poetry helps us to—"

"I ain't 'shamed," I say, looking back at her.

"Well then, why did you lie to your father about the book?"

I mumble some words.

"What did you say, Langston?"

"I said, 'Can't I have something all to myself?'"

"Like reading?" she asks.

"Like the library," I answer.

"Is that where you go after school?"

"Don't tell my daddy. He thinks I play with some boys after school."

"Well, I'm sure your father wouldn't mind."

"Please don't tell Daddy. I'll tell him soon. Just not yet. Not now…"

I'm gonna be late and Miss Fulton's gonna tell my daddy and he ain't gonna let me spend my days at a library.

"I'm gonna be late, Miss Fulton." I don't wait for an answer 'fore I take off running to school.

I'm just about calmed down 'cuz I made it to my class before the bell rang and that's when I see Lymon sitting in back of the class at his desk, smiling. At me.

"Take your seats please," Mrs. Robins says to the class.

Out the corner of my eye I see Clem, but he's looking like he didn't even see Lymon. I don't hear one thing Mrs.

Robins says for the next three hours till lunch. The class laughs when she calls on me twice to answer a question and I still have to say "Excuse me, ma'am?"

I find a quiet spot in the sun away from everyone else in the school yard. No sign of Lymon, but they don't usually bother me at recess.

Last night I almost made my way through each poet in the *Caroling Dusk* book. The cover says it's an anthology and when I asked Mrs. Robins what an anthology is, she said it means a collection. *A collection of Negro poets.*

I'm careful to look up and make sure no is going inside and I'm still alone. I made a promise to myself that I'd read every Langston Hughes book they have in the library. So today, I'm starting *The Weary Blues*. My daddy listened to the blues back in Alabama on an old scratchy record. Sometimes he and Mama danced but it just sounded to me like an old man crying about something he couldn't have. But Mama said the blues makes you feel the hurt deep down in your gut and the blues is about how much colored folks go through in life and love. Not something I'd want to dance to. I wonder what Mr. Langston Hughes feels about the blues. I flip though till I find a title I like and stop at one called "Poem 4: To the Black Beloved."

Ah,
My black one...

This one I think I read before so I turn the page to another called "Harlem Night Club." But that "Poem 4" stays in my head, even when I finish "Harlem Night Club." I turn back.

> *Thou art not beautiful*
> *Yet thou hast*
> *A loveliness*
> *Surpassing beauty.*

Just when I'm thinking again about that poem, I feel a shadow over me and look up to see Lymon, Errol, and Clem.

"What you doing over here all by yourself, country boy?" Lymon asks. He's smiling bigger than ever. I look at Clem but he looks away. "Bet you and your daddy thought I'd be gone for good, huh?"

I ain't in the mood for Lymon today and I don't answer like I know he wants me to. I just sit and stare up at him.

I notice he ain't much taller than Clem. I stand up tall.

Lymon snatches the book out of my hand and I go to grab it back but Errol pushes me into the fence.

"Give it here, Lymon!"

"Give it here, Lymon!" he says in a country accent.

"What's so interesting in this here book?" I know it ain't no real question so I wait.

He opens to a page.

"Yet thou hast a loveliness..." He messes up all the words and I laugh.

"What's so funny?"

"You can't barely read," I say.

"If I can't read, country boy"—I know I shamed him—"you can't neither." He holds the book to my face and rips out pages.

"No!" I scream.

And then he rips out some more and throws them into the air. The wind carries them across the school yard.

Lymon might as well have ripped my heart out right along with those pages. The library and Langston Hughes 'bout the only thing that kept me going without my mama. Now I ain't even got that. I never knew I could have a feeling so mad and so mean inside me. Madder than when Mama died and we moved away from Alabama. Madder than having to live in this city without her. It keeps growing till I feel it explode out of my chest.

My hand reaches out quick and grabs Lymon's arm, tight. Errol tries to pull my hand away but I don't let go. Clem runs yelling, "Mrs. Robins, Mrs. Robins!" but I still don't let go. Lymon's other arm swings at me but when his bony arm hits me I only grab tighter. The book drops to the ground and I still keep hanging on tight, till I see tears coming to Lymon's eyes. He spits in my face. He's hurting bad but we ain't saying anything, we just staring into each other's eyes, me with his spit running down my chin.

"Pick up my book," I say finally. But he don't move. I twist his arm a little till he drops to one knee.

"Let him go!" Errol yells.

"Pick it up," I say again. And he does, slow, staring at me all the while. Usually boys and girls scream and yell like they're at a Joe Louis match when they see a fight, but now everyone is standing around, staring back and forth at the two of us, quiet.

I stand him up and let go just as Mrs. Robins comes over.

"What is going on here, boys?" she asks, out of breath.

Neither of us says anything.

Errol starts, "Country b-b...Langston grabbed—"

"Both of you, inside now!" I've never seen Mrs. Robins so mad.

I snatch the book from Lymon and look around for the ripped pages. Not one of them in sight.

Walking behind Mrs. Robins, I wonder what Mama is thinking if she is looking down on me.

In my head I hear Lymon stumbling on those words, *Yet thou hast a loveliness*. And even though I can still feel the mad inside me and I'm on my way to the principal's office and I'm gonna get a whupping from my daddy, I smile because now I remember that was the poem Mama wrote in her letter to Daddy.

seventeen

I waited for Daddy to give me a good whupping. And when
he didn't do that, I waited to hear him yell. He didn't do that
neither. He sat me at the table and did something I never seen
him do. He looked me in the eye and said, "We gonna talk,
man to man."

It'd be a lot faster if he went on ahead and gave me a
whupping.

"You know you can't go fighting your way through life.
Colored man got a whole lotta hurt they facing every day, we
fight every one, we're never gonna get anywhere. Bible says
we—"

"Daddy…" I wanna stop him 'fore he gets too deep into
the Bible. "I know I ain't s'posed to be fighting, but Lymon just
keeps at me."

"You're responsible for you. Your teacher said there was a
book…."

I told Miss Fulton I'd tell Daddy about the library.
Might as well go on and do it.

"I found a library near the school. Hall Branch over on Michigan."

"A library?"

He don't yell so I keep going. "Libraries ain't just for white folks. This library is for residents. That means any folks that live in Chicago."

"I know what a resident is, son."

"Anyhow, I go there after school sometimes and get books."

"Thought you been playing with some boys after school," Daddy says, leaning back in his chair.

"They don't like me here, Daddy. And it ain't just Lymon. It's everyone."

"Maybe you need to stop going to the library and find some boys your age you can play with. You shouldn't be sitting up in a library every day."

"Library's the only place in Chicago I want to be," I tell Daddy.

Daddy thinks on that a minute.

"Why?" he asks.

"It's as quiet as Alabama. The librarian, Miss Cook, she's real nice. She picks out books for me too." I pull my books out of my satchel and hand him the *Weary Blues* book.

"What's this?" Daddy asks, turning the book over in his hands.

"I found this in the library. A book of poetry by a man named Langston Hughes. He's a colored poet."

Daddy still turns the book over in his hands like he don't quite know what to do with it.

"Remember how you and Mama used to dance sometimes to the blues?" I ask.

His lips turn up at the corners a little bit.

"Daddy. The library has all kinds of books. And these books by Langston Hughes remind me…of home and Mama."

"How's that?" Daddy asks, serious, still looking down at the book cover.

"Because he writes poems about being colored and living up North but missing the South and feeling lonely. Miss Fulton likes his poems too."

"Listen, son. I don't know anything 'bout Langston Hughes and I sure don't know anything 'bout any poems. Only Langston I'm worried 'bout is the one sitting here in front of me."

We're quiet for a bit.

"Can I read you one?" I ask.

"Read me a poem?" Daddy laughs.

"Just one," I say.

"Sure, go on and read me a poem."

I try to remember how Miss Fulton read the words, slow and strong. I open one of the books and start.

> *De railroad bridge's*
> *A sad song in de air.*
> *De railroad bridge's*

A sad song in de air.
Ever time de trains pass
I wants to go somewhere.

I stop and look at Daddy, but Daddy's just looking at his hands. I keep reading.

Homesick blues, Lawd,
'S a terrible thing to have.
Homesick blues is
A terrible thing to have.
To keep from cryin'
I opens ma mouth an' laughs.

Time I finish and look up, Daddy is just sitting quiet.

"Sounds a lot like the blues," he says finally.

"Yup," I say. "But don't it remind you of back home?"

"Your Mama...she was smart too. Head was always in a book," Daddy says, chuckling to himself.

"Mama liked to read?"

"Sure she did. She never got as much schoolin' as she wanted. After her folks passed, she moved from kin to kin and couldn't stay in one school long enough. But she had an aunt. Think her name was Genevieve, called her Aunt Gennie, lived up in Ohio and would check in on your mama whenever she came back home. And she always brought your mama books from up North. Tried to make sure she kept up her learning. First time I saw your mama she was reading...."

Daddy looks away for a minute, then goes on.

"Then when we got married, we had all we could do trying to keep up with planting and keeping house and then you came along. Wasn't no time for books."

I think of the letters in the box under the bed.

"Did Mama like poetry?"

"Don't think she knew much about poetry, but she liked to write."

I can feel the heat rise up to my face. Some secrets ain't worth spilling.

"Look, son"—Daddy stands up—"tomorrow you are gonna go and say you're sorry to this boy Lymon."

"Yessir."

"He bothers you again, you walk away, understand?"

"Yessir."

What about the library? I want to ask but don't.

Lymon don't scare me near what he used to. We learned a lot about each other in the school yard today. Only thing scares me is bringing a ripped-up book back to Miss Cook at the library.

eighteen

I woke this morning to the wind whipping against the window, so I shove Daddy's old gloves into my jacket pocket before I head to school. I'm surprised how fast I got used to the cold even though the wind makes me hunch up my shoulders and walk fast.

Both me and Lymon got detention after school today, so I'm gonna have to wait to go to the library. Not that I'm in a rush to tell Miss Cook I destroyed a book. I hope she don't take my library card away. If I think too hard on it, I'm gonna want to hurt Lymon all over again, so all the way to school I think about Mama watching and Daddy's man-to-man talk and the Bible to get the mad thoughts out of my head.

When I walk into the school yard it's the first time since I started I don't hear the name *country boy*. Some of the boys in my class even smile at me. Takes me a while to realize I musta done what they been wanting to do for a long while. Lymon's still gonna be Lymon, ain't no changing that. Just like I promised Daddy I would, I walk right up to him and say,

"Sorry, Lymon." He nods his head and walks away with Erroll. Clem is watching from the other side of the school yard. I'm still not sure what to make of Clem.

Detention is one whole hour. A man teacher, who looks mean as can be, sits at a desk in front while we sit in desks in a classroom not saying a word. Anybody says anything gets another day of detention. But this ain't nothing like library quiet. More like jail quiet. Half the older boys in the room I've never seen before and don't want to see again. Lymon knows a few, though.

When detention is over, I rush to get my books and get out of the classroom, but there's no need to rush today. Lymon's not even looking at me. He's talking to some of the older boys so I take my time walking down the stairs, through the school yard and back to the apartment.

I have some pennies in my pocket so I stop at the corner store for some candy. The bell on the door jingles as I open it and close it behind me. Inside it's dark and smells like cigarettes and mints. Mr. Jackson sits on his stool listening to the Cardinals and Red Sox game on the radio behind the counter, an unlit cigar hanging out the corner of his mouth. Boys at school been talking about the World Series. Seems in Chicago everybody's a baseball fan but me and Daddy. Even though I know exactly what I'm getting, I take my time walking up and down the case, running my hands along the wooden counter. Finally I grab a roll of Life Savers and put my pennies in Mr. Jackson's fat, sweaty hand. He puts the money in the register and reaches back to turn up the knob on the radio.

I look in the window of the shoe store next door wondering if Daddy's gonna be able to get me some new shoes 'fore the winter comes. Maybe even the boots they have in the window with shiny black leather and thick, strong laces. I seen pictures of snow in my schoolbooks, and I don't think my shoes are gonna hold up.

I get nods from the men standing in a group in front of a barber shop. At the corner of Forty-Third Street a newsboy holds out the paper, shouting the headline: *"Louis KOs Mauriello in record time!"*

"Can't no one beat the Brown Bomber," folks laugh as they pass, like Joe Louis is fighting for all us colored folks.

I remember the first time I walked home from school. I was so scared I'd get lost, sweat prickled under my arms. Everywhere I looked, folks looked like they were moving so fast I wondered why everyone was in such a hurry. Now I can't tell if folks have slowed down or I just sped up.

Up ahead I see Miss Fulton sashaying toward the building. I see some men tipping their hats to her face, then turning to look at her behind as she walks past. Miss Fulton keeps walking like she doesn't even notice but I can tell she does. She sees me too and waves hello and waits for me at the stairs.

"Well hello, Langston." She smiles. Ever since the week when Daddy went away, Miss Fulton is acting like we are bosom buddies. She's fine and all, but I'm not sure whether she's being nice because of Daddy or nice because of me.

"Hello, Miss Fulton."

"I was hoping I'd see you," she says.

"Ma'am?" I ask.

"I wanted to show you a new book of poetry I found. I thought you might like it."

"By Langston Hughes? 'Cuz I read nearly all the ones in the library...." I know I'm talking fast and excited, but I can't stop.

"Speaking of the library, did you ever talk to your father?" she asks.

"Yes ma'am," I say. "And he don't mind me going to the library." I don't know when lying started coming so easy to me. *I'm sorry, Mama.*

"Didn't I tell you he wouldn't mind?" she says.

"Yes ma'am."

"Well, I'll drop the book by tomorrow," she says at her door.

"Thank you, Miss Fulton."

The cold follows me into the apartment. Daddy says the landlord turns on the heat only when he's in the mood, so I guess he ain't in the mood today. I ain't allowed to light the stove, so I'm gonna be cold till Daddy gets home.

On my bed, I flip through the *Weary Blues* book and let my mind wander. In my daydream I see Daddy seeing Mama for the first time reading a book under a tree. And I see Mama writing in her fancy letters the words of Langston Hughes, word by word, in a letter to Daddy. I picture Daddy trying to make sense of those pretty words. He said he didn't know nothing about poems, but when he left everything else behind, he kept the words she wrote tied in a ribbon and brought them all the way to Chicago. She never told him that Langston Hughes made her heart sing the way he does mine. That she wanted to name her baby boy after the poet she copied in her letters.

I ain't got the heart to tell Daddy those weren't Mama's words. Seems like Mama left us both with her secrets and we bound to keep it that way.

nineteen

WALKING to school the next day, my satchel has the same amount of books but feels heavier than ever. I been practicing what I'm gonna say to Miss Cook, scratching out lines in my head that don't work. So far I got *Afternoon, Miss Cook. When I got home, this* Weary Blues *book had some pages torn out.* But that don't sound right, so I try *Miss Cook, my daddy got mad when I wasn't doing my schoolwork and ripped up this book.* But I don't want Daddy in trouble for something he didn't do. Daddy said a man's got to own up to his mistakes, so I'm gonna tell Miss Cook just what happened with Lymon and hope she'll forgive me. My stomach is hurting something bad but I got what I'm gonna say inside my head. Since Mama passed, I ain't much for praying. God let me down once before, but I bow my head and say a little something to God now.

All day at school I keep going over my speech to Miss Cook. When the bell rings at the end of the day, I'm not the first one to the door, not even the second. First time I ever walked slow to the library. Ain't no need to rush something you don't want to do.

Kicking leaves out of my way, I hear "Watch where you going" in front of me.

With my head down, I nearly bump into Clem standing in the doorway of the library.

I jump back. "Watch where you standing," I say.

"I been waiting here for you," Clem says.

"Why's that?" I ask.

"Thought you might be wanting these." Clem waves a fistful of pages over his head like he's waving a flag. The pages from *Weary Blues.*

I grab them fast. "These all of them?" I ask, flipping through.

"Yup. Every single one of them. Had to climb a fence to get the last one, but I got it." Clem looks real proud of himself.

"If your friend Lymon hadn't..."

"Lymon ain't my friend," Clem says.

"Since when?"

"He been getting on my nerves anyhow. But when he went and ripped your book...I'm staying away is all."

"Thanks for this," I say. "I was thinking Miss Cook's gonna take back my library card."

Clem laughs loud in my face. "Take back your library card? They don't do that. They mark the book damaged, maybe make you pay. Now that you got the pages they can fix it."

Clem can see I feel stupid thinking they take back the card. "I'll tell Miss Cook with you," he says.

Miss Cook is downstairs at the desk, filing cards into a drawer.

"Excuse me, Miss Cook," I start.

She smiles. "Yes, Langston. Oh, and hello, Clem." She looks a little surprised.

"I need to talk to you about this book." I hand her *The Weary Blues.*

"Yes," she says, staring at the cover.

"Well...I was in the school yard...."

"Kid from school named Lymon ripped out some pages, but I got them all. Show her, Langston." When Clem said he would help me tell Miss Cook, I didn't think he would do all the telling.

I show her the pages and Miss Cook gets a frown on her forehead.

"And these are all the pages here?" she asks me.

"Yes ma'am."

"Langston, a library book is your responsibility. And you are—"

Clem cuts in. "Wasn't his fault, Miss Cook, honest."

"Thank you, Clem, but as I was saying, Langston, when you borrow a book, it is your responsibility to make sure the book is returned in the same condition as when you borrowed it. This book will need to be repaired, but I think it can be done."

Even though Clem told me how the library works, and Miss Cook said the book can be repaired, I still ask, "So you're not gonna take back my library card?"

She smiles then. "Of course not, Langston. You are our number one patron." I sure don't know what *patron* means, but I like the way it sounds. *Number one patron.*

"Then I can check out more books?"

"Absolutely," she says, smiling again.

Clem goes off to get a new one of those books he's reading. I head back to poetry to get another book, and he waits while I check it out.

Upstairs and out on the sidewalk Clem asks which way I'm walking. "Over to Wabash," I say.

"I'll walk with you a ways," he says, not even asking if it's okay.

We walk a block without saying anything at all.

"What is *Weary Blues* about?" he says finally.

"Ah, just a book I took out."

"But Lymon was reading those words—*hast, loveliness*—what kind of book is that?"

"It's poetry," I say.

"Like *Romeo and Juliet*?" Clem asks.

I never read a poem called *Romeo and Juliet*. I shake my head no.

"What's poetry about?" Clem asks.

"Poetry's about a lot of things, I guess."

"Like *love* and *flowers*." Clem laughs, elbowing me in my side.

"Sometimes, I guess. But I like the poems that talk about other stuff."

"What is it you like about 'em?" Clem sounds serious, like he really wants to know.

"I like that it feels like...like someone is talking just to you. And that someone else knows what it feels like being... you. I can't explain it....," I say, feeling mad I can't say in words what I mean.

But Clem says, "You mean like the way you feel about Lymon."

"Kind of like that. But not just Lymon. The way I feel when I think about Alabama and my mama...."

"Your mama? Where is your mama, anyway? I saw your daddy when he came to the school."

"My mama passed." I don't say no more.

"My daddy passed." Ain't like Clem to say so little, so I wait. "That big explosion on the Navy ship in California? Port Chicago disaster, they called it. My daddy was on that. Been three years now...." He stops again. This time he don't say no more.

"Sorry, Clem. That why you want to go into the Navy? To be like your daddy?" I ask, scared he's gonna be mad, or worse, sad 'cuz I'm reminding him about his daddy.

"Guess so," Clem says. He don't seem mad. "Sorry 'bout your mama."

We stay quiet, crunching leaves as we walk.

"So the poetry you read is a way of putting all the things you feel inside on the outside."

"That's about it." Between all he knows about the library and getting my mixed-up words, Clem is a lot smarter than I thought.

"I gotta go up this way," Clem says at the corner. "See you tomorrow."

"See you tomorrow, Clem."

He didn't laugh. Didn't make me feel like a fool.

I walk on home thinking about poetry and Mama and Clem. My first friend in Chicago.

twenty

I'M feeling like this is about the best day I've had in a long while till I walk into the apartment. Miss Fulton is there at the table with Daddy, and when I walk in they look funny, like I just caught them at something.

"Hello, Daddy. Hello, Miss Fulton."

"Son," Daddy says.

"Hello, Langston," Miss Fulton says. "I brought you over that book we talked about."

Got a feeling that ain't the reason she stopped by, but I keep quiet about that. She hands me a book of poems called *Harlem Shadows.*

"Thank you, Miss Fulton," I say, wondering what Daddy's gonna say once Miss Fulton leaves.

"I'd better be going or I'll be up all night grading papers," she says to Daddy, smiling like Daddy is one of those actors in the picture shows.

Daddy walks Miss Fulton, *Pearl,* to the door and sees her across the hall. I watch him watch her and realize Daddy is looking at Miss Fulton same way the men in the street look at her when they tip their hats.

The door barely closes when I ask, "Daddy, you in love with Miss Fulton?"

Daddy makes a sound something between coughing and laughing. "No, son. She's a nice woman who's been neighborly to us is all. What's this book you got here? More poetry?"

"Um, yes sir. Miss Fulton said she thought I'd like it."

We stand in the middle of the room looking at each other. Man to man. Me waiting, Daddy waiting. I don't know how Daddy feels about the library and me reading poetry and me being smart like Mama. Don't know if he thinks that's a good thing or bad. And since he ain't saying much, I'm gonna guess it ain't good.

"I'm gonna get started on some supper."

"Yes sir."

"You made your apologies to that boy?" Daddy asks.

"Sure did, and he didn't say nothing. Just walked away."

"You just steer clear, you hear me? I don't want no more foolishness at that school."

"Yes sir."

We eat our supper quiet like always. I scrape the plates and wash up for bed. Daddy takes his towel to head to the bathroom. I lie on my bed staring up at the cracked ceiling, peeling all over. I close my eyes and see Mama, clear as day, smiling down on me.

I open my eyes, open my book, and start reading.

> *I would liken you*
> *To a night without stars*
> *Were it not for your eyes.*
> *I would liken you*
> *To a sleep without dreams*
> *Were it not for your songs.*

I hear Daddy at the door, stepping into the apartment. But for the first time, I don't put the book down, or hide it under my covers. I keep reading.

"Langston," Daddy says. And I hold myself tight, waiting for what he'll say.

"Yes sir." I keep my head in the book, making sure he sees me.

"Time to turn these lights out and go to sleep. Tomorrow's Saturday, and I don't want to hear any fuss in the morning about getting up 'cuz you were up all night reading."

"Yes sir." I can't help but smile. *That's all he's going to say?*

Time the morning sun comes through the window, I can smell the oatmeal and toast Daddy's making.

"Come on, son, we gotta get a move on," Daddy yells from the stove.

I shuffle sleepyheaded to the table. Toast ain't burned too bad this morning so I start with that. Daddy sips his coffee, looking at me.

"Gotta make an extra stop today, so I need you to hurry it up this morning."

"Where we going?"

"Don't worry about that. Just need you to get moving so we're not out all day," Daddy says.

Outside, the October sun is warm on my face and makes me miss the warmth of Alabama. Daddy is walking faster than he usually does so I struggle to keep up behind him. He nods at nearly everyone he passes and I do too. We make all of our stops—the bank, the landlord, the post office. I show Daddy the boots I saw in the window and he says he needs a little more time to put some money together 'fore I can get shoes. I hope my feet don't get frostbite in the snow while I'm waiting. That's how cold I hear Chicago gets in winter.

We get to the corner of State Street where we usually turn to go to the fish market, but Daddy nods his head in the other direction. I get to thinking how much I didn't know about my Daddy when we lived in Alabama. With Mama there, he barely spoke to me, and I didn't know what to say to him. But now, with just us two in Chicago, I know Daddy better than I ever hoped to. I know now he ain't in the mood for talking, so I walk right 'longside him, wondering where we heading. Trees pop up along the sidewalks and the run-down apartments turn into houses with nice cars parked in front and fresh-painted trim around the windows. We get to the corner and Daddy turns to me.

"Which way is the library?"

"The library?" I ask, not believing my ears.

"Want you to show me this library where you spending all your time."

Now I recognize the neighborhood. "Over that way." I point.

We cross the street and I can't help but realize that two blocks back I thought I knew my Daddy. Now I'm back to not knowing again.

When we get to the big wooden door of the Hall Library, Daddy looks around like he ain't so sure anymore about seeing the library.

"Wanna see inside?" I ask him.

I open the door and Daddy walks in behind me. In the entry, the bright October sun shines bright, warming the whole room. Grandma was right. I can feel Mama looking down on me. Daddy'll probably never know that in the letters he hid was a secret she kept. That she named me for a poet whose words she loved and kept hidden in her heart, just waiting for a baby boy. Maybe she knew she wasn't long for this world, knew I'd need something to get me through, but whatever it was, Mama led me to this library. Helped my hand reach out to a shelf holding a book with my name, and it saved me from the pain of losing her and from a city I hated. And Mama, all the way up in heaven, helped me along the way to finding home.

Author's Note

The road to Langston's apartment at 4501 Wabash Avenue in Chicago, Illinois, could never be found on any map. It winds through stories told by my mother-in-law, Margaret Williams, and my husband, James Ransome; through memories of my childhood summers at Aunt Ophelia's home in Charlottesville, Virginia; across the pages of Isabel Wilkerson's *The Warmth of Other Suns* and past the round wooden tables of the Malden Public Library in Massachusetts; along the Illinois Central Railroad and down the streets of Chicago's South Side.

Langston's story begins post-World War II in the fall of 1946. The economy is booming and factories are hiring recent arrivals from the South, Northern blacks, and men newly returned from the war.

Langston and his father are just two of the seven million blacks who migrated north during what is now called the Great Migration. From 1916 to 1970, Chicago's Union Station received more than five hundred thousand blacks who left the South in search of a better life in the North. Chicago's black population grew from two percent to thirty-three percent in just over fifty years.

The growing black population in Chicago grew the cultural scene as well, providing a home to musicians and singers such as Louis Armstrong, Cab Calloway, Muddy Waters, and Mahalia Jackson, visual artists Charles White and William Edouard Scott, and the writers Lorraine Hansberry, Arna Bontemps, Gwendolyn Brooks, Richard Wright, and of course Langston Hughes, all of whom formed the Chicago Black Renaissance.

Langston Hughes spent much of his writing life in New York City, but his brief time in Chicago was well spent. Hughes lived in the Hotel Grand at Fifty-First and South Parkway, and spent much of his time in the spring of 1939 at the George Cleveland Hall Branch library working on the first draft of his autobiography, *The Big Sea*. He later donated the manuscript drafts of *The Big Sea* to the Special Negro Collection at the library. He also wrote the Jesse B. Semple columns for the *Chicago Defender* newspaper. He, along with writers Richard Wright, Arna Bontemps, Zora Neale Hurston, Gwendolyn Brooks, and Margaret Walker, were featured speakers at the library's Book Review and Lecture Forum series, which was begun in the 1930s by librarian Vivian Harsh as a way to introduce the surrounding community to works by prominent writers of color. Vivian Harsh was Chicago's first black librarian and the first head of the Hall Branch.

Chances are, Langston would not have been able to visit a library in rural Alabama in the 1940s. Not only were libraries racially segregated, but of all the libraries in the state of Alabama, fewer than one-third were available to black residents.

The George Cleveland Hall Branch of the Chicago Public Library, where much of the story takes place, was the brainchild of Chicago surgeon and civic leader Dr. George Cleveland Hall. He was the second African-American to serve on the board of directors for the Chicago Public Library, and he made it his mission to build a branch in the Bronzeville neighborhood, the first of its kind to serve its community members and promote African-American culture and history. He enlisted the support of the NAACP, the Chicago Urban League, and philanthropist Julius Rosenwald, who donated land he owned at the corner of Forty-Eighth Street and Michigan Avenue. During its construction, Dr. Hall passed away and the board voted unanimously to name the library in his honor. On January 18, 1932, the George Cleveland Hall Branch first opened its doors to the public.

The Hall Branch has been called the Black Jewel of the Midwest, and today serves ten thousand visitors each month.

Lesa Cline-Ransome

Acknowledgments

Special thanks to my editor, Mary Cash, who saw a seedling of this story and watered it and loved it and helped it grow strong into a beautiful magnolia. And a loving thanks to my dear friend, Ann Burg, whose confidence, words, and guidance helped me find my way to novel writing and Langston.

And to my two favorite readers, James Ransome, who listened again and again to every draft, offering invaluable input and Leila Ransome, aka my Assistant Editor, who endured months of readings in my office when she tried to tiptoe past to her room. Her keen, youthful perspective, unfiltered critique and literary analysis helped to bring Langston to life.

The amazing team at Holiday House Publishers, thank you all—Terry Borzumato-Greenberg, Emily Campisano, Emily Mannon, Faye Bi and Derek Stordahl, and the rest of the HH family, for their continued support.

For the Malden Public Library and all the libraries and librarians who change the lives of children every day by leading them to books and opening worlds.

As always, thank you to my wonderful family—Linda Cline, Bill Cline & Darlene Azadnia, David Jennings, J.E. & Marlene Williams, Patricia Richardson, Tita & Leigh Carter, my mother-in-law Margaret Williams, and my saintly mom, Ernestine Cline, who showed me the transformative power of books.

My deepest gratitude for my cubs—Jaime, Maya, Malcolm, and Leila (and my snoring office companion, Nola), who always inspire, uplift, and motivate me to #keepgrinding.

FOLLOW LYMON'S JOURNEY FROM WARM, LOVING MISSISSIPPI
TO COLD, UNFAMILIAR NORTHERN CITIES
AND HIS FATEFUL MEETING WITH LANGSTON IN

Leaving Lymon

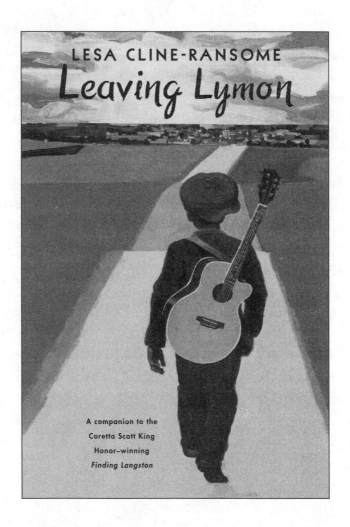

LESA CLINE-RANSOME
Leaving Lymon

A companion to the
Coretta Scott King
Honor–winning
Finding Langston